What Happened

Peter JOHNSON

Front Street
Asheville, North Carolina

The excerpt on page 6 from "How To Like It" is from *Velocities* by
Stephen Dobyns, copyright © 1994 by Stephen Dobyns. Used by
permission of Penguin, a division of Penguin Group (USA) Inc.

Library of Congress Cataloging-in-Publication Data

Johnson, Peter.
What happened / Peter Johnson. — 1st ed.
p. cm.

ISBN-13: 978-1-932425-67-3 (hardcover : alk. paper)
[1. Hit-and-run drivers—Fiction. 2. Fathers and sons—Fiction.
3. Interpersonal relations—Fiction.] I. Title.
PZ7.J6356Wha 2007
[Fic]—dc22
                          2006012028

Front Street

An Imprint of Boyds Mills Press, Inc.
A Highlights Company

815 Church Street
Honesdale, Pennsylvania 18431

For Kurt, Lucas, Kevin,
and my old buddies from Canisius High School

. . . How is it possible to want so many things
and still want nothing. The man wants to sleep
and wants to hit his head again and again
against a wall. Why is it all so difficult?
But the dog says, Let's go make a sandwich.
Let's make the tallest sandwich anyone's ever seen.
And that's what they do and that's where the man's
wife finds him, staring into the refrigerator
as if into the place where the answers are kept—
the ones telling why you get up in the morning
and how it is possible to sleep at night,
answers to what comes next and how to like it.

—Stephen Dobyns, "How To Like It"

What Happened

Part I

There are no facts, only interpretations.
—Friedrich Nietzsche

I don't know what the truth is, or who needs to hear it, but I know what happened, and if my story seems erratic it's because I think that way, because it's not as if one event happens, then another, everything following, like a parade, in a logical progression leading to a happy ending, because there haven't been many happy endings in my life or Kyle's, or happy beginnings or middles either, just events needing to be pieced together like a jigsaw puzzle, and if we can do that, then maybe we can make sense of those events and live with what we did or what others said we did. So listen: here's where my story begins, here's where my story ends.

"If you don't stop chattering, Pill Boy," Pork Chop said, his meaty face quivering with laughter, "we're going to tie a rope around your neck and drag you from the back of the car."

Duane laughed too, and when he gunned the engine I could feel the rear of the new BMW slide in the snow. It had been snowing hard for the last three hours without a plow in sight, but Duane didn't seem to notice. He grasped the steering wheel with his left hand and held a joint in his right, the hand he had punched Peter Respinis with, the one with a bloodstained handkerchief wrapped around it. "In Maine, they feel no pain," he sang, laughing, and Pork Chop laughed with him.

"What the hell is that supposed to mean?" Kyle asked.

"In Maine, they feel no pain," the two of them sang, Duane gunning the engine again, the car sliding sideways, then righting itself.

"Just take it easy, Duane," Kyle said, trying to grab the joint from his hand.

"If you want some," Duane said, "all you have to do is ask."

"No way does Kyle want that action," I said. "If you knew anything about Kyle, you'd know that."

"Who are you," Pork Chop said, "his old lady?"

"Lay off him," Kyle said.

"Or what?"

"Or I'll kick your big fat ass."

The last time I saw my father was the day we buried my mother. After the mourners left, he kissed me and Kyle on our foreheads and sent us to bed. He was a big, tall, handsome man, a high school basketball star, but that night he looked tired, his eyes glazed, unblinking. It had been one of those December days when you could smell snow coming, so cold I wondered how they could dig a hole that deep. I asked Kyle, but he said, "Go to sleep," and that's when I dreamed myself in the cemetery, reading the metal name tags tacked onto trunks of different trees—*Pin Oak, Japanese Zelkova, Cucumber Magnolia*—and wondering where the squirrels were, because they roamed freely when my mother and I did gravestone rubbings. But then I saw it, a red-tailed hawk, gliding toward me from the top of an oak tree, yet I wasn't afraid, holding my ground as it approached and bared its talons. I threw myself onto the ground at the last moment and felt a chill pass over me, then awoke to a loud scraping, the digital clock reading 2:04, my mother's glass paperweights staring at me from my nightstand. I looked toward Kyle's bed, but he wasn't there, instead crouched by the window overlooking the backyard, the garage light illuminating his face. "What's that?" I asked. "Shhhh," he said, "come here," and I crawled over to the window. It must have been snowing as we slept, and it was still coming down hard. In the driveway by the basketball stand, my father, in jeans, sneakers, and a white T-shirt, frantically shoveled loads of it behind him. Kyle and I watched for about ten minutes, but even as the snow let up, he kept shoveling until he had cleared a large area in front of the basket. He pressed the automatic garage opener, went inside, and returned with a basketball, then started shooting baskets, slowly at first, measuring shots, then tossing the ball away from him, tracking it down, turning and shooting again, and when he missed he'd charge the backboard, softly laying the ball in, on and on, running hard, jumping, dribbling, sometimes slipping or pausing to brush back his snow-wet hair. "Is he crazy?" I asked. "No, he's sad," Kyle said. "We should sleep now." And that's what we did. In the morning we looked everywhere for my father, but he was gone; all that remained were a wet T-shirt on the kitchen table and a pair of soaked basketball shoes drying by the radiator.

I live with my brother Kyle and my aunt Lucy on the North Side of Buffalo—not the wealthy section, where landscaping trucks full of Hispanics and Asians unload their rakes, lawn mowers, and leaf blowers. Not the section where long-legged Catholic and Jewish girls park their fathers' BMWs.

That's where Duane lives.

That's where his sister Emily lives.

I go to Canisius on a scholarship because my father went there, because my mother died, because I live with my aunt who teaches at an all-girls' school, because I'm smart and can play basketball, and because something happened a long time ago that makes people watch out for Kyle and me, though Kyle says he wants to be left alone. He's angry but doesn't take meds like me. That began in the fifth grade when I fell asleep at a school movie and woke up panting. There was a huge lion on the screen, part of one of those happily-ever-after movies I've always hated. Since then, I've seen that movie ten times, trying to understand what happened, but I've come to see that I'm just wired differently from most people. Sometimes I feel as if I have been touched by God or something like Him, and if I listen hard I can hear Him. He sounds like a blue jay squawking from the oak tree behind my house, like a basketball kissing a gym's hardwood floor, or a pan rubbed clean by a scouring pad, or maybe angry thunder in the distance, or the hush when I imagine Kyle kissing Emily, the hush, hush.

That's what it's like to be inside my head.

"A sensory overload of great magnitude" is how Kyle once described my brain as he hugged me close in the middle of the night.

And there was another night when Kyle and I were sitting on the base of the basketball stand in our driveway, Kyle spinning the ball on his index finger, watching it shimmer like a Christmas bulb under the backyard light. "Smooth," they call him, because that's how he moves with a basketball.

"Do you ever think about Dad?" I asked.

He grimaced, then stood and began shooting short jumpers.

"Well, do you?" I persisted.

"It's not important," he said.

"But don't you ever wonder if he's alive?"

"No."

"Why?"

"Because he's dead."

"How do you know that?"

"Because he's always been dead."

There were four of us in the car that January night: me, Kyle, Pork Chop, and Duane. We had beaten St. Joe's in the semifinals, so we went to Rondo's house to party. Rondo's parents were never home. We often wondered if they even existed, but no one complained because we could do whatever we wanted to with whoever we wanted to whenever we wanted to. And Rondo had a bowling alley downstairs. A real, professional bowling alley with an automatic pin-setter. Rondo's family took bowling seriously, and he used to collect bowling shirts from used-

clothing stores. In fact, you couldn't get into
this party unless you were wearing a bowling
shirt and bowling shoes, so there we were, about
thirty kids, drunk or stoned, rolling balls down
the alley or getting a running start, like Kyle did,
hurtling his lanky body toward the pins. It was
rowdy yet under control until Rondo noticed that
Duane and Pork Chop weren't wearing bowling
shirts. I'm not exactly sure what happened after
that because I started drinking, but I remember
Rondo and Duane pushing each other, then
couples pairing off and making out on couches or
in corners, and Peter Respinis was there, a straight
arrow, president of the Sodality, a nice guy, really,
but he shouldn't have gone to that party, especially
not with his girlfriend, because someone was
bound to start in on his name, and of course it
was Duane, idiotically shouting, "Peter's red *penis*!
Peter's red *penis*!" so that he had no choice but
to defend his honor, and that's when the party
moved outside, everyone grabbing their beers as
Duane and Peter squared off in the backyard in
jeans and shirts, all of us too drunk to care about
the snow. Maybe it was the cold or the snowflakes
melting on my face, but I started to come around
as the first punch landed. It was hard to believe
the number of punches being thrown, that
sickening sound of bone hitting flesh, and though

we wanted to break it up, we didn't. Kyle made a move once, but Pork Chop and some other guys held him back. The fight continued until Duane, most likely out of frustration, tackled Peter and began to pummel him, and that's when, out of nowhere, Emily, dear sweet Emily, broke from the circle and jumped on Duane's back, knocking him to the ground. They rolled over a few times in the snow, Duane's muscular frame ending up on top of her, melted snow and sweat dripping from his thick blond hair. And that's when Kyle broke free and jumped him. Now this was a battle we wanted to see, but it never happened because the rest of our team separated them, probably thinking about next week's championship game. After the fight we all calmed down, as if some ache had been relieved. Duane even offered to give us a ride home.

Emily is a fact, a force of nature. I first saw her when I was hired at CVS the summer of my sophomore year to stock shelves and sweep the back room. I don't know why she decided to work, since she didn't need the money. But I was told to ask her if I had questions, so I asked as many as possible because there was a kindness in Emily that drew me to her. At break time we ate protein bars and sipped Cokes while sitting on boxes of aspirins and laxatives. Emily had greenish blue eyes you could almost disappear into. She was a midfielder on her soccer team, tall and thin but strong and really cut. She wore tight solid-colored tops, though not to be flirtatious, and her broad shoulders made her breasts stand at attention, so it was hard not to stare at them.

One time, after a weekend morning shift, Emily asked me to go to the zoo, and I thought for a moment that maybe, just maybe, she was interested in me, but she wanted to talk about Kyle, and though she asked me not to tell him, I did, believing that was what she really wanted. We were just about to leave the monkey house, which was good because I couldn't watch this one monkey throw up and eat it one more time, when she said, "You know, my parents knew your parents in high school. My father even went out with your mother."

I didn't know what to say to that.

"My father played basketball with yours and they won the championship," she added.

That fact I already knew, though I had never met her father. There was a wing of classrooms named after him, but anyone can buy anything if they want to.

"Why does Duane hate Kyle?" I asked.

She seemed surprised. "Why do you say that?"

"Because Duane told Kyle to stay away from you."

She seemed angry and changed the subject as we walked to the habitat of the African Wild Ass, the animal I wanted her to see. I explained that it was one of the rarest animals in the world, a cross between a male ass and female horse, which was the truth. I also told her I was going to adopt it because the zoo had a program where they sent you adoption papers for any animal you helped feed. She laughed, but I told her I was dead serious, that I'd adopt every animal in the zoo if I could.

"Even the one who eats his own puke?"

"Especially," I said.

And she laughed, that big, beautiful Emily laugh. "You're nuts," she said, and in a way I am.

Pork Chop and Duane laughed crazily as the BMW continued to slide in the snow.

"Let's take a spin around Delaware Park," Duane said, veering off the main road next to the zoo, and when he did, any extra light from nearby houses disappeared, as did the road itself, so that Duane was driving from memory or what he had left of it. When we passed the entrance to the zoo, the right rear tire caught a curb, tossing me and

Kyle around in the back seat. Pork Chop dropped the lit joint onto the floor, and when it rolled back to us, Kyle grabbed it and threw it out the window, saying, "Jesus Christ, stop the car."

"He tossed the joint," Pork Chop complained, but Duane laughed.

"It's under control, Smooth," he said. "You know how many times I've made out on this street."

Kyle leaned over the front seat as if to grab Duane, but Pork Chop pushed him back.

"Relax," Duane said. "You don't want to get me mad. I'm already soaking wet from pounding Respinis, and I've got two losers in the back seat, one who's banging my sister, much to my dad's unhappiness, and in spite of all this, I'm fairly down with the night. I mean, it's a beautiful night for a ride."

Pork Chop laughed and lit another joint, passing it to Duane, who gunned the engine, the left side curb keeping us from skidding into a streetlight.

Kyle sat back, probably thinking it was best not to do anything until the car stopped, but Duane wasn't done talking.

"I read this book once," he said.

"I didn't know you could read," Pork Chop said, laughing.

"Shut up, asshole. Like I said, I read this book where this guy is driving ninety miles an hour, telling the people in the back seat he's going to smash them into a brick wall about thirty miles away. He's got it all planned and he's driving them nuts, asking them questions, and I like that idea, Smooth, so here are my questions: Why does my father hate your guts? Why do my parents still fight over your dead mother?"

But instead of waiting for an answer, he jumped the curb and drove us into the deep snow covering the baseball field. He was heading straight for the backstop, then swerved quickly, spinning us crazily in circles. It would have been fun if he hadn't mentioned that book and that brick wall.

"What's the deal, Smooth?" he asked, righting the car and heading out toward center field. "What's the connection?"

Father Samuel insists everything is connected, that there's one big cosmic plan explaining why plants grow the way they're supposed to and why the sun comes up every morning on time, "everything in nature and life," he says, "following some kind of logic." He calls this the Great Chain of Being, with God at the top, making all the decisions.

When he explained this in class, Rondo said, "Can I ask you a question, Father?"

"Of course, Mr. Rondelli. Didn't I make myself clear?"

"No, Father, I get what you're saying, but there's something I don't get."

"What's to *get*, son? It's all pretty obvious."

"Well, Father, Bill Sheehan—you know Bill, Father?"

"Yes, Mr. Rondelli, I know him."

"Well, he gave me a ride to school today, and on one of those radio talk shows, a news guy reported that in Eugene, Oregon, a guy killed his wife and mother-in-law because his mother-in-law talked his wife into having sex with another guy for a microwave oven."

A few students laughed, but Rondo didn't.

"No, I'm serious, Father," he said. "How do you tell this guy about the Great Chain of Being? I mean, how do you tell him that when God sat down to plan the universe he decided to have his wife mess with another guy for a microwave oven?"

This time everyone laughed except Rondo because he wanted to pull this off, to pretend this was a serious question, so that Father Samuel wouldn't knock him off his chair.

Meanwhile Father Samuel just stared at Rondo,

trying to decide what to do, because, like all of us, he knew that every Rondelli who ever went to Canisius was a wise guy, yet if this was a serious question he probably should answer it. So he explained that not everything can be explained and that this one incident was a part of a bigger plan, and it was curious to see him dancing around the question for ten or fifteen minutes, because all this was very funny, yet also very serious, because tell me if you can, how would *you* explain the Great Chain of Being to the guy, and if you can't, then what makes you get up in the morning?

Some nights I wake up soaking wet, thinking about the stupidity of it all, believing I will see my mother again but knowing I might not, fear suffocating me like a huge anaconda. Maybe I am afraid because my mother died or because my dad left us and then his parents moved to Florida and we never heard from them again. Or perhaps I'm the problem because there are people who are stronger than me who don't worry about every little thing, the kind of people who survive catastrophes but never ask why. I'd like to be them. I'd like to chuck my meds and all the quotations, lyrics, and fragments of conversation

I paste around the house to make me laugh or
remind myself not to jump off a bridge. But there
are times when clarity arrives, as if I'm looking
into a muddy pond and suddenly I can see golden
fish swimming below with answers flowing from
their gills. Usually these moments happen at a
tower downtown by the marina. Sometimes, after
school in the early fall or spring, I take a bus there
and buy two New York-style wieners, then sit by
the J-boats neatly anchored on shore. Afterward
I walk to the tower. No one is ever around, and
I climb four flights of stairs to the top, where I
can look out onto the lake and think about what
it must've been like to live here a hundred years
ago when people were too busy staying alive
to cause trouble. Things are complicated now.
That's why I come to the tower. Behind me, the
city—thousands of people twitching and cashing
their paychecks, all part of the Great Chain of
Being, not knowing that each link of the chain is
made of papier-mâché. In front of me, the lake,
its peace washing over me, making me believe
in something, I'm not sure what, but something.
"Believe, believe!" Emily once said to me, long
before the accident even happened.

Duane finally maneuvered the car back onto the road, and we rocketed out of the park. He was screaming and yelping, every once in a while banging his injured hand on the steering wheel, and when Pork Chop cracked a beer for him, it was clear there would be trouble up ahead: a cop, or maybe a huge snow-covered oak tree waiting for tragedy and the 6 a.m. news.

"Where're we going?" Pork Chop asked, a question I was thinking but didn't ask, fearing I'd make Duane more agitated.

"We're going to the Park Meadow," Duane said. "They won't check IDs this late."

So that's where we were headed at 2 a.m. with absolutely no one on the road, or at least so we thought, until we neared Parkside, when I heard, "Oh, shit," then a thud, and saw the blur of something—an animal? a man?—tumbling over the hood into the windshield. When I looked out the rear window, I saw a body somersaulting like a circus clown until it came to rest in the middle of the road.

"Oh, man, what was that?" Pork Chop said.

In this ending, no sun vanishing behind snow-tipped mountains while the all-American family huddles around a campfire cooking marshmallows, recalling the time Joe Bob Jr. saved Jasper the family kitten from Bruce the pit bull, or the time Missy Sue dished out mashed potatoes to the homeless on Thanksgiving.

For Kyle and me, always a different ending, each one beginning at a championship basketball game. According to this version, after throwing the ball into the stands, Kyle dresses and sneaks away while the cops and Emily's father try to track him down. He crawls through a locker-room window, Emily waiting for him in ankle-deep snow. She's wearing a blue parka, a short black leather skirt, and knee-high boots, her long blond hair whipped by the wind as her father's black Volvo idles in the parking lot. They tumble into it and pull away, their tracks quickly erased by snow. Kyle is thinking of another snowy night, and Emily's not thinking about anything except that she's with Kyle and that she'll never live with her father and Duane again, and it doesn't matter that they're only seventeen and that all they have between them is seventy-five dollars and twenty-two cents, because that's enough to get them to New Hampshire, where we used to vacation before my mother died. And though no one's crazy enough to be on the New York Thruway at 9 p.m. with visibility near zero, the Volvo carves its way across the state, passing rest stops outside of Rochester,

Syracuse, Utica, Albany, the snow letting up as they reach the Mass Pike, then past Springfield, through the outer suburbs of Boston, to Interstate 93, their final destination a little lakefront area outside of Plymouth, New Hampshire. It's 8:30 in the morning, and they've hardly spoken the whole trip, but now they look at each other and kiss, contemplating the ice-covered lake, sipping coffee they bought outside of Concord, Kyle thinking of the vacant cabin nearby, where they'll break a window and start a fire, curl up, and make love, knowing that tomorrow is already here. And when they wake there will be some kind of sign, maybe the sun reflecting off the lake, but more likely a big buck deer pausing five feet from the kitchen window as Emily hugs Kyle. The buck freezes, then shakes his head, his neck muscles pulsing from the weight of his antlers. He glances at them and leaps over a snow-covered wheelbarrow, vanishing into the woods. For you, it will be hard to believe that Kyle and Emily won't find hoofprints when they step outside to look for the buck, but for them it makes all the sense in the world.

"That was a guy," Kyle said. "You hit a guy, asshole."

The car had swerved off the road and come

to rest against a tree. Kyle kept trying to get out, but his door was wedged against the tree trunk. Meanwhile Duane was gunning the engine, rocking the car back and forth.

"What are you doing?" Kyle yelled.

"I'm getting the hell out of here," Duane said.

"I'm not leaving him here," Kyle said, trying again to escape.

"He's right, Duane," Pork Chop said. "Come on, man, we can't do that."

Duane took his foot off the accelerator. "Shit, look at the goddamn windshield," he said, referring to the nucleus of the collision surrounded by jagged circular cracks.

"Who cares about the windshield?" Kyle said. He was trying to crawl over me and jump out my door.

"You're not going anywhere," Duane said. "We're drunk and stoned. Do you know what'll happen to us?"

Kyle managed to escape but didn't get very far before Duane tackled him from behind. Pork Chop and I tried to separate them, all four of us rolling around in the snow. Behind us, the car idled peacefully; in front of us, under a streetlight, a body lay like a sack of dirty clothes. The pulling and shoving continued until we heard what amounted to a roar. We looked up and saw the haloed headlights and faint outline of a snowplow trudging down a parallel street. Duane broke from the group and ran to the car, turning off its headlights and silencing the engine.

"Everybody just shut up," he yelled.

Kyle ran to the shape in the street, and we followed. When he turned the body over, I heard a man groan and saw his bloodied forehead, a metal arm from a pair of eyeglasses sprouting from his left temple. At my feet I noticed what remained of the glasses and tried to position them on his face, the falling snow melting and mixing with his blood.

Duane pushed me onto the ground. "What are you doing, jerk-off?"

"Wait a minute," Pork Chop said. "I know this guy. He's the drunk who's always riding his bike in the middle of the street. Look," he said, pointing to a bike, nearly bent in half, resting about ten feet in front of the BMW.

"Yeah, he's a drunk," Duane said. "It wasn't my fault. He rode right in front of me."

"Just call someone," Kyle said, cradling the guy's head under his arm and telling me to use our cell phone. But when I said I'd left it at the party, he snapped, "Can't you do anything right?"

"We need to get out of here," Duane said. "Just lean him against a tree. He'll come to."

Kyle looked as if he was going to make a run at Duane.

"Okay, okay," Duane said. "I'll call, but the phone's in the glove compartment. Come on, Pork Chop."

"I'm okay here," Pork Chop said.

"No, come on. I want you to help me move the bike."

Pork Chop followed Duane, leaving me and Kyle with the guy.

"Are you drunk?" I asked Kyle.

"What?"

"Are you drunk? Because maybe Duane's right. When he makes the call, maybe we should just leave."

Before Kyle could answer, we heard the engine of the BMW turn over and saw the car rocking back and forth, dislodging itself from the tree. Kyle let the man's head fall into the snow and ran toward the car. "Asshole," he yelled, shaking his fist as the car sped off. The last thing I saw was Duane's left arm and middle finger extended skyward.

Facts

*The cold wind of a Buffalo winter, the shovel that will
    break the heart of the man who wields it,*

the snow at morning, the snow at evening, the bird
  stranded all winter on the frozen branch of our
  maple tree,
the hot oatmeal cooling on the kitchen counter, the swirl
  of maple syrup giving it taste,
the "don't" in "Don't be afraid," the "be" in
  "Be terrified,"
the city bus driver who takes us to school, who loves his
  wife and little girl, who recites the gospel at mass, who
  eyes Emily's ass as she steps off the bus,
the oldest lion at the zoo, the newborn panda, the sickly
  kangaroo,
and my mother's hand, scratching my head as I fall
  asleep, the promise she will be there when I awaken.
Don't be afraid. Don't be afraid.

Part II

But when you think you made it disappear
It comes again, "Hello, I'm here," and
I've got angst in my pants.
            —Sparks, "Angst in
                    My Pants"

"What do we do now?" I asked Kyle. The snow was letting up, but it was still cold and all I had on my feet were the red and black bowling shoes Rondo had lent me, whereas Kyle had changed into his work boots at the party.

"We have to call someone," Kyle said, walking back to the guy, then taking off his pea coat and laying it on top of him. "There's a pay phone by the Park Meadow. Just stay here. If you're gone when I come back, you'll be very sorry."

"I'd never do that, Kyle."

"Yes, you would. You wouldn't want to, but that's the way you are."

"That's not true."

"Christ," he yelled, "just stay put," and he vanished into a cloud of blowing snow.

I stood over the guy, trying to decide what to do. I knelt and touched his face, then tapped his cheek a few times. I thought I could awaken him before Kyle got back, but then got to thinking Kyle might not come back, then got to thinking this guy might wake up and out of fear or rage try to strangle me, then got to thinking everyone would blame me for this unfortunate turn of events, everyone would take care of their own sorry asses and I'd go up in flames, and at that thought I jumped away from him as if he were a poisonous snake, and if I could've found a place to bury him or erased the memories of anyone who'd ever met him, I would gladly have done so.

I wanted to run, just like Kyle said I would.

I wanted to rip a piece off the guy's bicycle and keep smashing it into a tree until Kyle got back.

I wanted to start shaking him, or to scream into his lifeless, alcoholic face, "It's you. You're the one we've all been waiting for."

But I knelt down again and rearranged Kyle's pea coat, gently rubbing the man's legs, then brushing the snow off his pair of beat-up running shoes, as if making him presentable for the autopsy.

"Believe," I said to myself. "Believe."

After my mother died, I stopped believing in anything for a while. I was the last to be told about her illness, though I should have seen it in her sunken cheeks, her smell, something like the odor when you unwrap a dead pig in biology class and begin to cut. She would sit at the kitchen table, helping me with math, while the cancer had its way with her, offering us just enough hope to make her seem noble and heroic. At the wake they praised her strength and faith, but I knew they thought she was pathetic and I hated them for having witnessed her trudging off to work, pale and bloated, as if infused with chalk, wearing an absurd black wig that made her look like a transvestite, my father insisting she was beautiful without it, Kyle just plain absent as much as possible. And where was I? I should have known. Someone should have told me. A person, or the Almighty, All-seeing, Everlasting God, the one Father Samuel talked about—He should have explained The Plan to me, told me why the Great Chain of Being was suddenly missing a link. I might have said or done something to alter events. I might have made a difference. "You're my baby," she often said to me, and more than once my father said, "Don't call him that."

Rondo thought my father was cool because he looked like Clint Eastwood.

Kyle says, "Why do we have to go over this again?"

Aunt Lucy maintains, "Whatever anyone tells you, your father loved you."

Father Samuel preached, "Your father will find peace in this world or the next."

"A loser just like you" was Duane's take, right before Kyle punched him in the mouth.

And me? I need to remember his face, to understand his absence, to mull it over, as if rubbing a piece of hard clay between my hands until all that's left is a pile of dirt.

Believe.

And for once it worked, Kyle appearing in front of me as if by magic, the snow letting up, Kyle soaked from head to foot, his long black curly hair glued to his scalp. He grabbed his pea coat and put it on, visibly shivering underneath it.

"Now we can go," he said. "The cops will be here soon."

"Shouldn't we wait?"

"We've done what we're supposed to do," he said.

We propped the man against a tree, then ran as best we could past the broken bike toward a stone wall about four feet high. We hurdled it and trudged along for a while, then stopped. Crouching down, I opened the top of my coat and wedged my hands under my armpits.

"Why are we stopping?" I asked.

"Just wait," Kyle said, turning toward the scene of the accident. He looked concerned. "Come on, come on!" he said.

A few moments later two police cars pulled up, red lights flashing.

One car unloaded two officers, who ran to

the body. From the other car, a man dressed in a topcoat appeared. He looked at the silent shape sleeping in the snow, then said something to the officers that we couldn't hear. He walked toward the bicycle but stopped before he reached it. He bent down and fingered the snow, then looked in our direction.

"Shit," Kyle said.

"What?"

"Our footprints."

I felt him push me from behind.

"Just stay low," he said, and we ran, sometimes slipping, sometimes falling down. We ran from the accident and from a siren chasing us down like a bloodhound, until Kyle tackled me as we were about to reach Parkside, realizing the siren wasn't from a cop car but an ambulance that would surely have tattooed us if we hadn't stopped.

"Cross here," Kyle said after the ambulance passed. "Just stay on the street where they've plowed. The footprints will end there."

And that's what we did, jogging close to the curb, hoping we could cover the six blocks home before anyone saw us.

Last summer I had another anxious night. Unable to sleep, I snuck out of the house and caught

the last bus downtown. I headed for the tower,
avoiding a few drunks and panhandlers. Most
everyone had left the waterfront for the night,
except for a few stragglers at a lakefront restaurant
and a few people partying on their boats. Bits
and pieces of conversation mixed with the
slapping waves and created a strange language. I
approached the tower, hoping no one was there.
I didn't hear a sound as I climbed the four flights,
my heart pounding. When I reached the top, I
looked out onto the water and felt a little peace
but not much, because that's how it goes with
me—sometimes everything shifting into fast-
forward, me not wanting to take a pill or to smoke
the joint Rondo had given me but to let the
anxiety wash over me. That night the rush was
so intense, I collapsed into a ball and pressed my
back against the cool concrete wall. I don't know
how long I sat there before I heard voices below,
footfalls ending at the first level. There seemed to
be about four guys my age, arguing over splitting
some cash one had stolen from his uncle. The
argument continued until one kid, obviously
the leader, said, "I'll break the neck of the next
motherfucker who says another word," and they
all went silent. If these boys discovered me I knew
they'd hurt me, maybe stick a knife into my heart.
Nevertheless, I almost screamed out, inviting

them to do their worst, until the fear of real pain silenced me, its adrenaline rush strangely settling my brain.

After they left, I decided to stay there for the night and deal with Aunt Lucy and Kyle in the morning. It seemed like a good idea, but then I heard footsteps again on the first level, then the second, then the third, until the intruder was about five feet away.

It was Kyle.

"Do you know what time it is?" he asked.

"Don't be mad," I said.

"I'm mad for Aunt Lucy, who decided to look in on you tonight."

"She'll understand."

"Of course she will, but that doesn't make it right." He sat down next to me and said, "What's going on?"

I wanted to explain but needed him to think I was stronger than I was. He wrapped his arms around me, and I began to cry.

"You think way too hard," he said. "So did Mom."

Was I like my mother? People always said so, but I never saw her indecisive or anxious or depressed, or even very angry. She was a nurse, something her parents didn't understand. Why become a nurse? Why marry a guy from South Buffalo, a steelworker's son? Why have two kids before she was twenty-two? And they never forgave her for marrying my father, making it clear that they planned to leave their cash, their house, everything they owned, to the Catholic Church, the thought of my father spending a cent of it more disgusting to them than my mother and her children living comfortably. As Rondo always says, "Dude, people are just totally whacked."

But not my mother. She believed deeply. In everything. Especially in some innate goodness we're all supposed to have. Kyle hated this kind of inspirational mumbo-jumbo. In the fourth grade he was sent home for punching a kid who threw water at him, and when my mother went to pick him up, the teacher told her that boys like Kyle eventually ended up in jail. It was a stupid comment and my mother knew it, but she explained to us that it wasn't worth arguing about. It would have just added negativity to an already negative world. As usual, all Kyle said was "Yeah, yeah, yeah," despite the fact that he, like my father, believed that even the smallest battle should be fought.

Still frozen from the long walk home, we found ourselves halfway across the living room when a light came on. Aunt Lucy was sitting in the recliner, looking half-asleep with a blanket draped over her knees and cradling a cup of coffee. She sighed deeply.

"I'm really trying here," she said. "Can you explain why you're shivering in the living room in your underwear at three in the morning?"

Kyle said he could, and I was eager to hear the story.

"First, go upstairs and take hot showers," Lucy said. "I'll make some tea."

We were half-naked because we had stripped and thrown our wet clothes down the basement stairs so we wouldn't leave a trail of water through the house. The rest of the explanation would be harder, but at the dining room table, sipping hot green tea, Kyle related how Duane had given us a ride home, how his car had broken down near the zoo, and how we didn't want to wake her, so we got home as best we could.

"At least you didn't have the Mazda," she said. "All I ask for is a phone call."

I said that I had left the cell phone at the party.

"What party?"

Kyle nudged me. "Rondo's party," I said.

"I'm not sure I want to know more," she said.

She was angry, and I could see my father's face in hers—the same blue eyes and square jaw, the way her face came to a complete stop when she was upset, suggesting she knew more than she was telling. I sometimes felt I had known Lucy in some previous life where she had been chosen to take care of us in this one, but Kyle said if that were true, then we were certainly a punishment and not a reward. She had been married once, but her husband divorced her when he discovered she couldn't have children, and I remember my father saying he was going to "tear the guy's heart out," which made me wonder how he could've abandoned us all, which made me further wonder if he had contacted Lucy but asked her, for some reason, not to tell us. She looked frustrated as she sat at the table. "I want to say one more thing," she said. "Duane is trouble, pure and simple, and you guys aren't getting that. Also, about half an hour ago, the phone rang four or five times, and when I picked it up, the line went dead. What's that about?"

Kyle and I both shook our heads.

"I'm really trying here," Lucy repeated.

"We know," Kyle said, placing his hand on hers. "We'll do better, you'll see."

In this ending we need a hero. Kyle hasn't shown up for the game, yet everyone believes he will, everyone except me and Duane, who have seen our fate in the crystal ball of a man's bloody face. But unknown to everyone, Kyle and Emily are sitting in a Dunkin' Donuts fifteen miles away. Kyle is staring at her in disbelief, and she's crying, saying, "He's my brother, he's my father, he's my brother. Oh, Kyle, I just want this to end." "But we can't do that, can we, Emily? You have to tell the truth." "Which is what? Whatever I say, you'll all be in trouble anyway, so don't make me do this." "But I wasn't driving. Duane told you so." "He's my brother," Emily repeats, and Kyle remembers a summer afternoon in Emily's house, her father's last words being "Emily will do what I tell her to, and don't think she'll ever live with you in some shit hole somewhere. She's not like your mother." *She's not like my mother*, Kyle thinks, grabbing Emily's arm as she tries to leave, then releasing it, looking at the clock, aware it will take him an hour to reach the gym if he decides to return because he can't drive there with Emily. Not now. And here is where you expect Kyle to catch a bus. You're with him as he watches the snow accumulate outside, snow on top of snow on top of snow, day after day, thinking how easy it would be to escape, but he's on his way to the gymnasium, stepping off the bus and running down the sidewalk through the entrance where a teacher asks for his ticket until she recognizes him and lets him pass. And it takes only a few minutes to change and be on the bench, the roar deafening as word of Kyle's arrival spreads, and there are just two minutes left when he enters the game, Canisius down by six points until he buries two three-pointers, then makes a steal and heads for the basket, and although he has never been tall enough to dunk the ball, he leaps from the foul line, and something like the hand of God lifts him over the rim where he jams the ball through as time expires, and even Duane is there to help him onto his teammates' shoulders while the cops wait outside, ready to tell us that the drunk has recovered and taken blame for the accident, no harm, no foul, and let's get on with the celebration . . . but that would be your ending with all kinds of sappy emotional props, while in fact, in reality, in truth, or at least in the truth of this ending, Kyle, broken by Emily's betrayal, doesn't leave Dunkin' Donuts in time to play in the game. But I do, and although we lose, I play hard for both Kyle and my father, even though the cops are waiting to question me again, even though I know Duane's father will take care of us and make sure Kyle gets off easy if I lie and say he was driving. I play hard, as if nothing is wrong. I play with my father's intensity and rage, yet under control, trying every move Kyle ever taught me, and you might ask what's heroic about that, and I'll tell you: I am not afraid. For the first time in my life, I am not afraid.

But it was fear that kept us up the rest of the night, knowing there wouldn't be news of the accident until the morning paper arrived or the morning news came on, so Aunt Lucy was probably surprised to hear us moving around at 6 a.m. on a Sunday. She was probably surprised to hear the TV on and the phone ringing.

It was Rondo. "What's with this cell phone?" he asked. "It just keeps ringing." He sounded as if he had a very bad cold, but then he always sounded like that in the morning. Pot can do that to you, and Rondo smoked so much, his sinuses were probably fried to the bone. "It just keeps ringing, man, and when I answer it, the dude hangs up."

I gave him my password and asked him to check the messages. While I waited, I watched TV with Kyle. The big story was the weather, the reporters doing what they always do, standing outside in the lake-effect storm telling us what we already know, that it's cold and snowing. Rondo came back on the line.

"The dude was Duane, talking some very crazy shit, that you guys better shut up because his dad's taking care of everything, and that he's going to keep on calling until you get back to him, and he keeps yelling, 'We've got to get this straight, Smooth, we've got to get this straight.' Is he talking about the fight last night? What's the big deal?"

I was about to tell Rondo what had happened but then heard Kyle yell, "Oh, shit," so I told him I'd call him back in a few minutes.

"Fuck that," Rondo said. "I'm going back to sleep."

I'd known Rondo since grammar school. Both his parents were alcoholics but very successful. His father was a judge, his mother a lawyer, but having two parents who are alcoholics is like having no parents at all, so what better friend for me than Rondo. The first time we spoke was the day I saw him walking on his hands. We were doing calisthenics in gym class, part of some citywide initiative to fight obesity in kids, everyone struggling with sit-ups and pull-ups while this big fat gym teacher called us wimps. Suddenly, fed up with the screaming and grunting, Rondo broke for the wrestling mat and did a handstand, walking around on his palms like a chimpanzee, a trick demanding incredible strength, even though he was fairly small and still is, one of those dark Italian kids who grew facial hair before the rest of us discovered thin strands under our armpits, and who fooled around with girls before we knew what that meant. Rondo was also the first guy I smoked pot with. He always knew where to get it, and I wondered if he was ever completely straight from the time he took his first toke, which was one of the reasons Kyle didn't like me hanging around with him. Kyle thought Rondo was a hopeless stoner, and he sure looked like one, his thin black hair now shoulder-length, always covered with an assortment of ski hats, his earphones so ever-present you wondered if he came out of the womb wearing them. He would never say what he listened to. Everyone assumed it was rap, but I think it was Bach or Beethoven, Rondo's way of thumbing his nose at people, and that's why I liked him. He read a lot and didn't care what anyone thought. And in spite of the weed, he was a good athlete, a cornerback on the football team. A kid once told me that in practice Rondo hit him so hard he thought his back was broken. One day, when I asked Rondo why he played, knowing he hated coaches and team sports, he said that the only time he felt truly alive was when he hit someone while they were running a crossing pattern. "I actually try to hurt myself," he explained. "In fact, you could say I try to kill myself." Rondo had also figured out his future. Having decided that it made little sense to study, he wanted to be the guy who chose the music for restaurants and grocery stores. "You have no idea how music can mess with people's heads," he said. "Give them Frank Sinatra one minute, then a flute-ensemble cover of Nirvana the next, and they'll end up leaving the store with Italian sausage instead of granola."

On the TV, in a clip apparently filed shortly after our accident, I saw a reporter in a dark topcoat and bright red ski hat. I almost yelled out, "I was there, I was there," but realized it was nothing to be proud of. Behind him a few attendants were hauling a stretcher through ankle-deep snow, loading it into an ambulance parked next to a cop car. Quarter-sized snowflakes were swirling like moths around the reporter and attendants, as if this scene were being played out in a huge glass snow globe God had suddenly picked up and shaken. The reporter said there had been a hit-

and-run accident. He said the victim was so far unidentified. He said there were few clues, since the snow had quickly covered up any tire tracks and footprints (which we knew was a lie). He said that the deed seemed "almost unthinkable and cowardly," adding that it was hard to believe "something so cold-blooded could occur in Buffalo." Of course, he didn't see Kyle cradling the guy's head, or me rubbing his legs, or Kyle risking frostbite to call the cops, or both of us waiting around until they arrived.

After the newscast, Kyle went upstairs. I heard him throw up in the bathroom, then Lucy say that if he got drunk again she'd have to ground him. He apologized, and I heard our bedroom door shut. I decided we should talk, but upstairs I found him curled up on his bed, his eyes closed.

"Are you awake?" I asked.

He nodded.

"Rondo said that Duane's been calling and wants to talk to you."

He nodded again.

"Aren't you going to call him back?"

He shook his head. "I'll talk to Emily when I get up."

I tried to stretch out on the twin bed across from him. On my dresser, I saw my apple paperweight, a rust-colored glass apple trapped

inside a clear glass ball. It was a gift from my
mother. I reached for it and hugged it to my chest.

"Can we go to jail for this?" I asked.

"Just go to sleep," he said. "Wait until I talk to
Emily."

That summer night in the tower, Kyle had
forgotten to tell me that Emily had come with
him, so I was shocked and embarrassed when I
saw her waiting by Aunt Lucy's Mazda. It was a
beat-up 1995 626, the butt of many jokes, even
some told by Lucy, but it got us where we wanted
to go. Emily was sitting in the passenger side with
the door open, listening to a classic-rock station.
She wore a red crewneck sweater and a short black
skirt, so when she stood up I glimpsed her inner
thigh. She turned off the radio and walked over
to us in a pair of red flip-flops, hugging Kyle,
then me. Kyle grabbed what remained of a six-
pack from the back seat and led us quietly over to
a barrier of huge boulders that kept waves from
washing onto the park. He held Emily's hand, and
she held mine. I kept waiting for someone to say
something. The restaurant had closed and even the
late-night partyers had crashed, so all you could
hear was the soft splash of fresh water massaging
the shoreline. Behind us, the sky was reddening.

The isolated outline of my fortress, framed by huge concrete city buildings, momentarily frightened me until Kyle handed Emily and me a beer, the hiss from the pop-top breaking the silence.

"Are you going to get into trouble?" I asked Emily.

"No," she said.

"Won't your parents be pissed?"

"They get so drunk on weekends, they won't even know."

"But Duane will be pissed," Kyle said.

"But he won't say anything. I know too much about him."

"Which I hope you'll tell me someday," Kyle said, laughing.

After I'd sat in the tower all night, the beer tasted good, and it made me want to smoke Rondo's joint, but then Kyle would've asked where I got it, and things would've gone downhill. As we sat there, the day slowly coming into being, I'd like to say we discussed our mixed-up lives, referring to dead philosophers and theologians, but, in fact, we drank quietly, Emily resting her head on Kyle's shoulder, until they strolled hand in hand toward the tower and disappeared into its entrance. I looked out onto the lake, missing the smell of Emily's perfume, envying Kyle because I knew Emily was his drug, her presence somehow injecting sense into the daily stupidities of his life, and I imagined my Emily, whoever she might be, right now sleeping soundly at home without realizing that within days or weeks or months she would fall into my world and save me. I mentioned this imaginary girl to Rondo once, and the next day he handed me a disk of pornography, telling me that my dream girl was "right there on that disk," and that I could take my time finding her.

At around 2 p.m. I woke up scared, hugging the paperweight to my chest, the pills and alcohol from the night before wearing off, every nerve in my body coming awake. One of my prescriptions would do the trick, but I didn't want to be stoned for the next two hours. My various shrinks could never figure out the right dose, and tired of being treated like a laboratory rat, I saw them as little as possible, learning how to medicate myself, realizing as time went on that I was beginning to tolerate the mood shifts better, so much so that they were like family, and even wondering if I'd miss them if some morning I woke up to find myself happy as a jaybird with smiley-face decals plastered all over our bedroom.

Fat chance! is what Rondo would have said.

Kyle wasn't in bed, but I could hear him talking downstairs, so I knew Lucy must have gone out. I got dressed and joined him.

"His father wants to see us," Kyle said.

"What?"

"He wants to talk to us."

"I thought you were going to call Emily."

"I did."

"What did she say?"

"She said to talk to her father. She was acting very weird."

"What do you mean?"

"Jesus, what does it matter? He wants to talk to us, so we'll go. We have to do something."

"We can tell Lucy."

"No, we can't tell Lucy, and we won't because Duane's old man said he can take care of this and no one will get hurt or into trouble. All we have to do is talk to him, so that's what we're going to do."

I reminded Kyle that the last time we saw Duane's father Kyle had told him to go fuck himself.

"Yeah, I remember."

Snow Globe

A glass snow globe, tossed from hand to hand,
As if someone's making a decision.
To drop it? To throw it against a brick wall?
So hot inside, the snow burning like white ash.
And it's always snowing.
That's me, my feet glued to the base of its bulb,
So I can't see the juggler's face.
But he's having a good time,
His laugh like the roar of an engine
Powering a crooked plan.
I'm standing in the hot snow,
Waiting for a girl to place me on her dresser.
To whisper, Believe, believe.
But in what?

Part III

I have discovered that all human evil comes from this, man's being unable to sit still in a room.
—Blaise Pascal

On the way to meet Duane's father, I wondered
if this was all a dream, and thought that if it was,
then maybe we could dream hard enough and
make it go away, make the drunk disappear, bring
our parents back, watch God-like from above as
Lucy's ex-husband awakened in some cheap motel,
realizing he'd abandoned the best woman on earth.
And as we turned onto Emily's street, I explained
all this to Kyle, waiting for a hint of recognition on
his face, but he just laughed. "You know," he said,
"you should be a poet when you grow up."

"Why do you say that?" I asked, knowing that
Kyle wasn't aware I wrote poems.

"Because no one ever knows what the hell
you're talking about."

The first time Kyle told Emily's father to go fuck
himself was last summer, when I began working
at CVS and Kyle started dating Emily. Kyle had
the Mazda that early evening and was driving us
to a summer basketball league at Delaware Park,
but he had promised to take Emily to work,
so we stopped by her house. He'd already told
me Emily's parents had asked him to beep the
horn and wait in the car when he arrived, but
he walked to the front door and rang the bell
anyway. Emily wasn't ready, and I could see Kyle

fidgeting on the porch when a large man opened the door. The next thing I knew, Kyle was waving for me to join him.

We followed the man—he must have been six-eight—through a huge foyer into a room with a pool table in the center and comfortable padded leather chairs and couches off to the left near a wet bar. The walls were decorated with pictures of him posing with politicians and professional golfers, and it became clear to me that rich people probably called this the "billiards room." He was holding what appeared to be a large glass of Coke. When he faced us, I took a good look at him. He was dressed in chinos and a blue polo shirt, white leather loafers on his sockless feet. He was overweight, so seemed even larger than he was, and he was sweating in spite of an overhead fan groaning above us. Still, he was handsome, his blue eyes made brighter by the contrast with his reddish gray hair. He looked powerful, like those politicians on the wall.

He strolled over to the wet bar. Without saying a word he scooped two ice cubes from a small stainless steel bucket and dropped them into two glasses. He poured some Coke, offering the glasses to us. "That's all we have," he said. "I drink rum and Cokes." Then he pointed to a leather couch, adding, "Sit over there." We obliged, and he grabbed a well-worn leather chair and slid it across from us, then sat on its edge. He was no more than two feet away, and it was clear he wanted it that way. His face was sun-damaged, his eyes tired. He looked at Kyle and shook his head. "We've never really talked, have we?"

"Not unless you've been in the car with me when I've waited for Emily."

"A wise guy, heh. Your father wasn't a wise guy. Just the opposite. Probably too nice. It's a weakness, you know."

"I really just came to pick up Emily."

He seemed annoyed Kyle was speaking without permission. "Well, she's obviously not ready, so let's chat. We can talk about your father."

"I have nothing to say on that subject," Kyle said.

"What about you?" he asked, looking at me.

In fact, I did want to talk about my father. I always wanted to hear anything from anyone about him. But I knew this wouldn't please Kyle.

"He doesn't want to talk about him either," Kyle said. He moved as if to stand, but the man grabbed his shoulder and guided him back onto the couch.

I could feel Kyle's anger at this gesture and was afraid to look at his expression, knowing he was about to explode.

"Well then, let's talk about basketball," the man said. "I heard you're pretty good."

"I do all right," Kyle said.

"But I'll bet you're not as good as your father. Back then, no one was, though he never knew when to shoot. We almost lost the championship because he always had to pass to the open man even if the dickhead couldn't make the shot."

"Dickhead" was not a word I expected to hear from him, and I realized he was a little drunk.

"I didn't like your father very much," he confessed.

"Neither did I," Kyle said.

The man laughed. "I liked your mother, though. Everyone did. She was an extraordinary woman. What a waste."

When he mentioned my mother I became anxious and asked where the bathroom was. He motioned toward the hall leading upstairs, and I left the two of them alone, hoping that when I came back I wouldn't find Kyle standing over him with a bloodstained pool cue in his hands.

It took me a few minutes to find the bathroom, and what a bathroom it was. It had a skylight and two marble sinks, all sporting gold-plated fixtures. There was a shower and next to it a marble bathtub. Over the sinks was a wide rectangular mirror into which I stared. I set down my Coke

and ran cold water, splashing some onto my face.
Then I sat on the toilet seat, staring at the bathtub
across from me. This was probably where Emily
bathed, since her parents most likely had their
own bathroom off the master bedroom. I thought
of her undressing and sliding into the tub, then I
thought of Kyle having a bad time in the billiards
room, then of my mother and father, and an old,
familiar dread started to rev up its engines. I
walked back to the sink and grabbed my Coke.
Then, for some reason, I opened the medicine
cabinet and spied a few bottles of pills. I spun one
in my hand, not bothering to read the label. I
don't know why, but I emptied its contents into
the toilet, flushing down a quantity of large red
capsules. I recapped the empty bottle and placed it
back in the cabinet, then left the bathroom.

When I reached the corridor leading to the
billiards room, I noticed that the party had
expanded. Standing in the hall were Kyle, Emily's
father, Emily, and a middle-aged woman, who
was beautiful the way a model is beautiful—
expressionless, with rose-petal lips and a porcelain
complexion. She was leaning seductively against a
stretch of ornate purple molding, holding the stem
of a half-filled champagne glass, with a cherry
floating in it. She wore tight yellow Capri pants
and a tight white top, and in spite of her age, she

had the ass of a teenager. Her blond hair was cut short, which highlighted her huge green eyes. When she looked at me I felt an urge that only her daughter—for it was clear that Emily was this woman's daughter—had been able to elicit.

"And who are *you*?" she said. She seemed amused by my sudden appearance.

"We're out of here," Kyle said to me.

Obviously something had gone wrong while I was away.

"No," Emily said, "I don't want to go. I want to know what you said to him, Daddy."

"I didn't say anything," her father protested.

"What did he say?" she asked Kyle.

"It's not important," he told her.

"But it is," she said.

"You sure you want to know what he said?" Kyle asked Emily.

"It seems we have a little drama here," Emily's mother interjected cheerfully. Emily's father seemed just as amused as his wife.

"He said he'd give me a summer job at one of his dealerships and four new tires if I stayed away from you," Kyle said.

"Oh, Daddy," Emily complained, while her mother laughed and said, "This is getting interesting," and her father added, "Well, I guess you can go, now that you've had your say."

"Yeah, yeah, yeah" was all that Kyle replied.

"Can't you do better than that?" the man taunted.

"Why don't you just go fuck yourself," Kyle said, then led me and Emily toward the door.

Just before we reached it, Emily's mother said, "Wait," and when I turned around she was standing next to me. She touched my chin and turned my face gently from side to side. She was so close I could smell her perfume and the liquor on her breath. For a brief moment, her smile disappeared into what looked like sadness. "You look just like her," she said.

I was about nine when my mother first took me to the cemetery. It had small grassy areas where you could picnic, as long as you didn't camp too close to the monuments or disturb the visitors. My mother was a nature lover and enjoyed pointing out different species of flowers and trees that landscapers had strategically arranged around the graves. Our favorite spot was near a dead Edwardian family, a series of gravestones with lifelike representations of the people buried there, mostly children sculpted to look like angels with their arms crossed over their breasts. Next to the children's gravestones, as if watching over them, were the graves of their parents and grandparents.

My mother had asked me to carry a plastic gallon of water while she lugged a large canvas satchel, which she opened, removing a scroll of thin paper and emptying out black crayons, masking tape, a scrubbing brush, a few rags, and a pair of scissors. She pointed to one particular gravestone and carried the equipment over to it. The inscription read *Elizabeth Thayer, 1836–1866*. The name was surrounded by flying birds, and underneath the name was a hand apparently in the motion of chopping. My mother said that the birds represented the flight of the soul and that the hand was God's, cutting her life short. She pointed out that Elizabeth's three children had died the same year, which suggested that some disease had taken them all. I asked her where Elizabeth's husband was buried, but she didn't know.

She grabbed the brush and gently scraped the gravestone, explaining we had to be gentle or we'd damage it. She poured water over the stone and wiped it clean with a rag, then went back to the satchel, opening a different pocket and retrieving a few candy bars, which we ate while the monument dried under the bright sun. We lay on our backs, staring up at the sky and giving names to passing cloud formations, my mother asking me what I wanted to be when I grew up.

I said I didn't know, and she said that was the best possible answer. When we finished the candy bars, she taped a thin piece of paper to the gravestone and rubbed a large black crayon over it until the name and carvings appeared. I can still see her taking a deep breath, rolling up her creation and clutching it to her chest. I can still recall her satisfaction and a strange kind of recognition—of what I'm not sure—and for a moment I felt we might suddenly sink into the earth, disappearing among the gravestones, and that it wouldn't be a bad thing.

Duane said, "If you have to be a hero, we'll all end up going down for it."

Duane said, "Just don't give him a bad time. Don't piss him off. You know he can take care of this."

Duane said, "Think of Emily and what this will do to her."

Duane said, "Smooth, you know we're not that different. You know there's some respect there."

Duane said, "If you screw this up, I'll beat your ass. You can count on that."

And I wondered which Duane was the real one, thinking back to a story I'd heard about Kyle's first week of high school. Duane and his rich friends had taunted Kyle, something about the way he was dressed, not having the right tie or shoes, and Duane was probably onto something, since Kyle didn't care about clothes. More than likely, from playing basketball against Kyle in the summer leagues and from hearing our mother's name invoked at home, Duane knew he would have to compete with Kyle. As the story goes, Duane started in on some skinny kid who'd gotten a scholarship for winning a spelling bee, and when Duane and Pork Chop tried to stuff the kid into his locker, Kyle stepped in. Some say he and Duane exchanged punches, others that Kyle slammed him against the lockers a few times, but whatever happened set the pattern for the next year when I arrived and for the two years after that.

Duane was big-boned, thick-lipped, blond, and handsome, like those magazine models with deliberately disheveled hair whose white enamel smiles glance playfully at us, suggesting privilege and money. There were a lot of guys like Duane at my school, but they didn't have Duane's eyes, which weren't the aquamarine of a warm sea rimming a tropical island but the ice blue of the deep where sharks hunt. Duane wasn't evil because of something he was; he was evil because of something he wasn't. In a past life, he would have been the centurion who pierced Jesus' side just as the sky exploded with rain and sadness, and rather than being terrified by this sign, he would have smiled heavenward as he walked down Golgotha.

Rondo once tried to write a novel about evil, which began, "Evil! Evil! Evil!" but he couldn't come up with anything after that. "Why?" I asked. "Because once you've said 'evil' three times, there's nothing left to say." Rondo also thought Kyle should have taken the tires. "Four tires isn't bad," he said. "If it were me, I would have asked for the whole car, then picked up Emily and banged her in the back seat."

We were talking about this in the cemetery one day, smoking dope and throwing a knife into a tree, but that's another story. Sometimes events overlap inside my head, like two live wires, and I'm not sure when something happened or if it happened at all. For instance, there's the story about a girl I followed off the bus one day, or maybe it was a dream. Every day she'd board the bus at the stop after mine. By the way she was dressed—casual clothes, no briefcase—I figured her for a secretary just out of high school, but her beauty guaranteed she wouldn't work for long.

Instead, she'd marry some young guy on the rise looking for good genes and end up living in Emily's neighborhood, which made me both want and hate her. But for now she seemed deeply sad, and I wanted to help her, imagining us living in a little apartment on the West Side, making love every morning, then hanging out in coffee shops, trying to shut out the world and all its punishments. But I never said a word, just watched her as she stared out her window, never smiling, never frowning. One gray winter morning, still semidark at seven-thirty, I saw her reflection as she gazed out that window, and for a moment I thought she saw mine. I was sitting on one of the benchlike seats, staring at her long red hair draped over the neck of her blue raincoat. The bus was crowded, and after offering my seat to an old guy, I braced myself on another seat, not more than four feet from her, so close I could see her eyelashes open and close. My stop was coming up, but I had no desire to get off, and wouldn't have except that a man brushed against my backpack and nearly knocked me over, which made the girl glance up. For a moment all I could see was her face—freckles, so many that she seemed to have a tan, and lime-green eyes, inquisitive and forgiving as a child's, as if she knew I had been staring at her. I was so rattled I got off at the next stop and walked three blocks to school, and for the rest of the day I was unable to shake her image. I knew I had to make a connection, but I didn't know how, until one morning, sitting in the back of the bus, lost in the shine of her hair, I decided to skip school and follow her. It was spring, one of those gloomy periods when the wind blows in one cloud formation after another, people beginning to doubt that the sun even exists. She got off downtown and went into a coffee shop not far from City Hall. I hung outside a few minutes, then entered, stopping at a rack of free magazines and paging through one of them. She was at the counter, purchasing coffee and pastries, which was obviously one of her pre-job duties. She paid the counter girl and walked toward the exit. I folded my magazine and stuffed it into my back pocket, hoping to reach the door before she did, but I got there too late. The girl left, crossing the street to where the bus had dropped her off, and before I could follow, she disappeared through the revolving doors of a large office building. I went back to the coffee house and waited, reading my magazine, getting hyped on coffee. Every half hour or so, I would strap on my backpack and try to walk off the caffeine buzz, cars speeding all around me, creating the whoosh, whoosh, whoosh of a machete. At one point I realized I'd

forgotten to call school with a fake excuse, but
I must have believed this adventure was worth
whatever punishment awaited me, because hour
after hour passed and she never came out for
lunch. What would I have said to her anyway?
I'm the guy who can't leave the house without his
pills, the one whose father loved his grief more
than his children, the one who would eventually
abandon a wounded guy in the snow because, as
Kyle said, "We did what we were supposed to do."

One thing we shouldn't have done was go to
Emily's house. We should've told Lucy what
had happened, then driven to the police station
and confessed. Certainly people would have
understood that we'd panicked mostly out of fear.
But instead we headed toward Emily's, the rest of
the world moving unquestioningly to my rhythm
for once.

When Emily answered the door, Kyle reached
for her hand and she offered it limply to him. She
was pale and seemed shaky. "They're all in my
face about this," she said. "Duane's story is very
different from yours."

"You don't believe me?" Kyle asked.

"All that matters is what *he* believes."

"Duane?"

She laughed. "No, my father."

"But you believe me, don't you?"

"Yes," she said. "But he wants to talk to you. To both of you."

Emily closed the door behind us, and I could hear balls colliding as we walked down the hall and into the billiards room. Her father was concentrating on his next shot.

"Where's Duane?" Kyle asked.

"Duane doesn't need to be here," Emily's father said, driving a yellow ball into a side pocket, circling the table, then looking up at us. He wore gray pants, oxblood loafers, a blue blazer, and a white shirt open at the neck. He seemed animated. A plan needed to be formed, people needed to be controlled and consequences avoided, and he was the man to orchestrate it, cheered on by the pictures hanging on the walls.

"I'm not saying anything until you get Duane down here," Kyle said.

Emily's father calmly placed his cue on the table and walked toward Kyle. He rubbed his chin, emitting a slight wheezy noise. He raised his right arm as if getting ready to chop Kyle in two, then lowered it. "You're not listening," he said. "Duane wasn't in that car last night and neither were you. In fact, after tomorrow that car will no longer exist. Do you understand what I'm saying?"

I thought this was why we came, so I was surprised when Kyle said, "What about the drunk?"

"What about him?" Emily's father said. "He's a casualty. He happened to be in the wrong place at the wrong time. That's what life is, being in the right or wrong place at the right or wrong time. Obviously, you guys haven't figured that out yet. Neither did your father, so maybe it's a hereditary thing. You all seem to have a talent for fucking things up."

I was actually relieved when he said he was going to take care of the accident, and I even agreed with his theory on being in the right place at the right time, but his last comment was bound to anger Kyle, and, to be honest, if he had included my mother in his evaluation of my family, I might have hit him with a pool cue.

"Do you understand what I'm saying?" he said.

Kyle seemed to be mulling things over, probably finding it hard to process the "talent for fucking things up" line.

"Yeah, yeah, yeah," he said. "I understand."

"So this is what we're going to do. We're going to forget the accident and walk out of here like three old friends. I'm going to give your brother a ride home, and when I come back, I'm going to give you the keys to my car and some money to take Emily out for a nice lunch somewhere."

"Your car?" Kyle said, mostly to himself.

"Yes, my car. I'm beginning to think you might be taking a step into the real world and leaving Loserville, so maybe we should try to be friends. As you said, we have one thing in common. We both didn't like your father."

I was waiting for Kyle to say something and having trouble catching my breath, as if every nerve in my brain had come awake. The longer the silence, the louder the noise between my ears, until I heard a voice, very much like my own, say, "From what I can see, you and Kyle don't have one fucking thing in common."

They both looked at me, as surprised as I was by the outburst.

In this ending, the image of an apple in a glass paperweight lying on the floor. The camera zooms in to reveal a smudge of human blood, so thinly layered it's almost transparent. As the camera retreats, the paperweight is given shape by objects around it—a bed, more paperweights on a nightstand, and, oh, yes, a body on the floor. It's Duane, like a big buffalo, suddenly brought down. I hit him because he came uninvited looking for

Kyle, because he snuck upstairs and crept up behind
me with a knife, because he called me Pill Boy
one too many times, and because he was going to
stop Kyle from going to the police, not knowing
Kyle had left two hours before to meet Emily. And,
yes, maybe he didn't have a knife, maybe it was
some other weapon or none at all, but it doesn't
matter because, in a sense, it wasn't even Duane
who showed up, but Fate with his vacuous, glacial
eyes—which is the last image I remember before
I hit Duane with the paperweight, surprised it
took only one blow, surprised his expression never
changed as he collapsed onto the floor, surprised
by my sudden calm as I dropped the paperweight
and sat on my bed, as if some strange prophecy had
been fulfilled. Yes, in this ending, I'm gazing into
Duane's dead-fish eyes while five miles away the
game has begun, Kyle wondering why we never
showed. He's already gone to the police station
with Emily, confessing to his part in the hit-and-
run, describing how Emily's father had the BMW
destroyed and was in the process of transferring
Duane to a boarding school. And because the
drunk hasn't died, the detective tells Kyle to go
home and stay put, but, of course, Kyle needs to
be with Emily, so they leave the station and spend
the afternoon at the zoo, walking from one frozen
exhibit to another, sipping coffee in the restaurant,

going over the events of the week and planning for the future, knowing that Emily's father will never forgive her. And eventually Kyle makes his way to the game, and here's where you can imagine the rest. Will he make the winning shot? Will it matter? Will you even notice the faint shadow of my father sneaking out the back door as the final buzzer sounds? Will you recognize him from the way he moves, from his height, from his habit of walking away again and again?

"What did you say?" Emily's father asked.

"I said I don't think you and Kyle have one fucking thing in common."

Kyle looked at me and laughed. "Let's get Emily," he said.

"You're not going anywhere," Emily's father yelled.

"What are you going to do, shoot me?" Kyle said.

"You better be careful," Emily's father warned.

"You going to offer me some more tires?" Kyle added, starting toward the door until Emily's father cut him off. Losing his patience, he grabbed Kyle by the arm, then let go, trying to regain his composure.

"Remember one thing," he said. "I can make

you and this little twerp disappear faster than your old man did. I owe the memory of your mother only so much."

And there was my mother again, brought up in the strangest context, as if I had been listening to a conversation but missed its true meaning.

"What does my mother have to do with this?" I asked.

"You really don't know, do you?"

"Let's go," Kyle said. "He's just jerking you around." And we left the billiards room in search of Emily.

I often wonder about my mother's last dream. I imagine her in the small room next to Kyle's and mine, nothing on the white walls but a clock face with no hands—her idea of a joke, one my father would never understand. She enters her dream by staring at a buttonhole on her nightgown, by yanking on the stem of a feather protruding from her pillow, by wishing herself into the face of that clock. In my mother's dream she has all her hair, which smells like oranges and lights up the night like a newly formed star. In my mother's dream the sun has turned her skin to butterscotch as she runs across a nameless cemetery or sometimes a beach with giant melting Popsicles sprouting from the sand. In my mother's dream the cemetery has no gravestones, no trees, and no hawks because it is composed of clouds, which she drifts on, never leaving her room, even when she dies.

Kyle was yelling, "Emily? Emily?" as he prowled the corridors of her house. I followed, glancing behind, expecting to see her father stalking us with a pool cue, but he was nowhere in sight. We walked through a living room, then into a kitchen, where a small Asian woman smiled at us while chopping little pieces of meat on a cutting board. She motioned to an opening, a small room off the kitchen, from which a stream of sunlight poured. We were nearly blinded when we entered the room—a cross between a solarium and a lounge—carved in glass, half of it decorated with an Oriental rug, comfortable furniture, and a small wet bar, the other half consisting of three-tiered tables that bore the weight of a number of exotic plants. Leaning up against the wet bar was Emily's mother, looking like a flamingo in tight pink pants, a white silk top, and one shoeless bare foot lifted behind her. She wore red sunglasses and was sipping a drink, the toenails of her bare foot burning like tiny flames. She stared at us, not saying a word, and for a moment I both hated and pitied her beautiful, cool indifference. She could have been some ancient ice queen battles were fought over, or just some pretty woman with a sad story selling toaster ovens on the QVC channel.

"Where's Emily?" Kyle asked.

She shrugged.

"Do you know what's going on here?" Kyle asked.

She shrugged again.

"Jesus Christ," he said, walking back toward the kitchen.

I lingered a moment with Emily's mother, not saying anything. I was about to leave when for the second time in ten minutes I surprised myself. "You knew my mother, didn't you?" I asked.

"You're the one, aren't you?"

"Which one?" I asked, thinking back to the drunk laid out in the snow.

She lowered the bridge on her sunglasses to see me better. "She told me you were her baby, that she loved you both but that you were her baby?"

"You knew her that well?"

She shrugged again, repositioning her sunglasses, then turning her back to me.

"Can I ask you something?" I said, but she either didn't care or was too drunk to respond. It was as if she periodically appeared in the house like a piece of furniture, though she must

have known something about the accident
and her husband's plan. Her silence made me
uncomfortable, so I felt for a tiny pill I keep
hidden in the watch pocket of my jeans, and I
stood there frozen to the ground until the weight
of a hand fell on my shoulder. It was Kyle.

"You okay?" he asked, leading me out of the
bright light back into the kitchen.

For a brief time after leaving Emily's I felt
strangely alive. With one statement to Emily's
father I had put something in motion, given a
huge stone its last nudge before watching it tumble
downhill. I would still do what Kyle wanted, but
I had made him see the horror of conspiring with
Duane and his father, and now we'd have to find
some other way to shoulder that stone back into
place. Without taking a pill, without obsessing on
a course of action until my head hurt, I felt I had
improved life somehow.

"What are we going to do now?" I asked Kyle
on the way home.

"I'm not really sure," he said.

"Do you think he meant that stuff about
making us disappear?"

"No, he was just trying to scare us."

"Do you think he made Dad disappear?"

He laughed. "No, Dad made Dad disappear. Just don't let him get into your head. You did good back there. It was funny to hear you swear." He tapped me lightly on the shoulder.

"But what are we going to do?" I asked again.

"I'm really not sure."

Snow

The Lord said, "Let there be snow," and the sun and moon turned their backs to us, while the first few flakes tapped lightly on windows, thickening on lawns and driveways into drifts through which people lugged their frozen "I's" past the black torsos of trees pockmarked by snowballs, past messages written on fences with snow, past lawn ornaments frozen to the ground, the snow obliterating names on tombstones under which the dead shiver, listening to the wind howl, "Don't expect miracles," before it drives the storm over baseball fields, a golf course, cages where animals huddle while their keepers breathe heat into their palms, and somewhere far away the sky so clear that planes fly just above treetops, children waving to them, struck dumb by the sky's blue immensity.

Part IV

Pooh looked at his two paws. He knew one of them was the right, and he knew that when you had decided which one of them was the right, then the other one was the left, but he could never remember how to begin.
—A. A. Milne

It didn't take long for a woman reporter to take a special interest in the accident, and within two days Kyle and I learned a lot about the drunk, who hadn't always been a drunk. At first we just had facts.

His name was Austin Clark.

He grew up in North Buffalo and attended Nichols, a local private high school.

He was a track star who went to Princeton and to Yale Law School, then returned home to practice.

He got married, and he and his wife had children—three daughters.

Then his personality began to emerge.

He lost one daughter when she ran in front of a bus ten years ago.

He began to act erratically, drinking and using drugs, once being admitted to a mental hospital.

His wife left him and he started to live on the streets, but never far from home.

He was arrested for violating a restraining order his wife had taken out against him.

Finally the portrait was complete, two pictures of him on the front page—one from his high school yearbook, the other with his family vacationing at their lake house shortly before the death of his daughter. The whole family was sitting on an empty picnic table in shorts and

T-shirts, suntanned and smiling. His daughters appeared to be in their middle or high school years.

So there it was: a face, an actual human being. Kyle and I never said so to each other, but the man's physical presence, the fact that he breathed, ate, made love, and worshipped, was one undeniable fact that would crush the fantasy of this accident going away.

"Believe, believe!" Emily said, hoping her generosity of spirit would heal the man's wounds, having faith that good things happen to good people. Sometimes I hated that flicker of naiveté in her, partly because I wished I had it, mostly because of its uselessness. Let's face it, most people are "good," in the sense that they don't try to run down others or abduct and eat them. But how does "Believe!" help me open my eyes each morning or follow my shoes out the door? I wanted to shake her and say, "What does that mean, Emily?" I wanted to say, "I tried to believe in you, but all you wanted was Kyle, so here we are, with everything to lose, and what do *you* have to lose, Emily?"

But like Kyle, I loved her, so I tagged along when she convinced him to visit a church the day after Austin Clark's picture appeared on the front page. We hadn't been in this particular Catholic church since my mother died. Aunt Lucy never went to mass or spoke about religion, as if she had outgrown God. But here we were, the three of us, late afternoon, in an empty church, which was cold as a meat freezer. When we first entered, we walked down the main aisle, then drifted off to a smaller group of pews toward the right, as if hiding from the huge crucifix on the altar. A fading sun brightened a stained-glass window, bathing us in crimson light as we sat staring at a miniature altar in front of us. I was waiting for Emily or Kyle to do something, but we seemed to have forgotten why we came. Should we kneel down in unison and ask for forgiveness, even though Austin Clark was still alive? Should we join hands and wait for a miracle? I sure had a long list of them, beginning with the resurrection of my mother. Oh, how I wanted to believe in something at that moment, but unable to do so, I felt as if I were taking a glimpse into Duane's black heart, wondering if anything mattered. I felt faint and looked up at the ceiling, trying to steady myself. It was framed with long, curved wooden beams simulating the belly of a whale, and that was how I felt, like some modern-day, hyped-up Jonah, going on a journey to nowhere. I was momentarily distracted by someone coughing near the main altar. A priest with long gray hair materialized like some medieval wizard, and I realized he'd been watching us the whole time. We held our breath as he approached and stopped outside a confessional booth, which he quietly entered. Right then, we could have taken turns confessing our sins and accepting divine penance, but we acted as if Mr. Death himself had shown up, the confessional about as attractive as a coffin, and we couldn't escape from that church fast enough, nearly slipping on its icy steps on our way to the car. The sky was beginning to darken, the smell of yet another snowstorm in the air.

I told Rondo the whole story, ending with our going to church, and he laughed. He didn't think running down Austin Clark was funny, but he couldn't understand why we didn't go to the police and get it over with, but then he hadn't been to Duane's house, didn't realize that Duane's father wasn't going to allow that.

"There's something else going on here," Rondo said, adjusting his earphones, "like some big goddamn Greek tragedy, you know, where there's a simple problem, but by the time everyone gets done complicating it, the world's not right for a couple of generations."

"I don't know what you mean," I said.

"Neither do I," Rondo said, "but there's something wrong with this picture, and I don't think God is going to take a break from making all this snow to straighten it out. If you want to think about a real God, think about that one. While we're all trying to live our dumb-ass lives, He's busy making snow." He laughed. "That's the guy Duane's father should be making disappear. That's the guy you should be shaking your fist at when you go to the tower. Keeping vigil with Sister Emily isn't going to help. I can guarantee that."

He turned up the volume on his CD player, vanishing into its music.

Maybe Rondo was right about our failed vigil, but Kyle had begun a vigil of his own, one I wasn't aware of until the fourth day after the accident. Until then we hadn't spoken much about that night, though we read the newspaper and watched TV. We went to school like zombies, ate lunch like zombies, walked by Duane and Pork Chop like zombies ("What're you going to do? What're you going to do?"), even practiced like zombies, Father Samuel yelling at us, once throwing a chest pass into Kyle's face. Although the championship game was only three days away, we might as well have been preparing for the school play. We were winded from worry and lack of sleep, our legs heavy as cannons, guilt beginning to weigh us down, sorrow waiting in the wings. I could see Kyle slowly losing it. He hadn't seen Emily since the day in the church, he wouldn't return her messages, and he would disappear for an hour or two after dinner. When he returned he would be very quiet.

One night I asked where he was going and he took me with him. We borrowed Aunt Lucy's car and drove to a traffic circle not far from school. We parked the car and headed toward a towering hospital, eventually getting sucked into its revolving doors. There were a number of soft chairs lined up where people waited for loved ones to be cured or die, which was exactly what Kyle had been doing.

"Sometimes I just sit over there," he said, pointing to a chair by the window. "It's quiet at night, no one checking in or out. Last night I spoke with an old Asian couple who were waiting for their granddaughter to give birth. They asked me why I was here, and I invented a bizarre story."

"What story?"

"I told them Dad had taken me ice-fishing on

a little pond in Hamburg and that the ice broke and I went under. I even described how it felt to be looking up at the sun from under the ice and how I kept reaching for the hole but couldn't find it, until Dad jumped on the ice, breaking through and saving me, and how I recovered quickly but because Dad was older he got pneumonia and was still very sick."

I laughed. "That sounds like something *I* would've made up."

"Yeah, I know. But I have that nightmare a lot, only no one saves me, and I wake grasping nothing but darkness."

"I have that nightmare, too," I said. "I call it my life."

As we left the hospital, I thought of my mother, how, at one point, she had probably lain in a bed not far from Austin Clark's room, until she decided she wanted to die at home. But Clark was still alive, so there was a ray of hope, and obviously Kyle thought his presence at the hospital might transform that ray into a full-blown rainbow.

Looking back, I wonder what my father would've done, though I'd have had a better chance guessing the reactions of a TV character, since I never spent

much time with him, or if I did, I don't remember.
There were days in the backyard when we'd
shoot baskets, but he was always more interested
in Kyle's game. I rarely recall him smiling, even
on vacations in New Hampshire, though his
brute physical presence seemed to soften around
my mother. I remember her scratching his head
while they watched TV; I remember him liking a
certain blue shirt patterned with white sailboats;
and I remember being roused one night by noises
and stumbling upon him and my mother slow-
dancing in the living room to some outdated soul
ballad. He looked surprised and disappointed, as
if I'd caught him being human. I often thought
he would've been happier if we didn't exist, that,
to him, we were a necessary, annoying part of
the deal, but how could I trust my memory of
those years, which had become as faded as one
of my mother's gravestone rubbings. Even when
we were young, Kyle said that when our father
died we would say, "Who was that masked
man?" but now we weren't even going to have
that final joke. So what would my father have
done? Something physical, I know that much.
He wouldn't have trusted in Fate or God or in
the innate goodness of his fellow human beings.
From the very beginning, he would have gathered
Austin Clark in his arms and walked him to the

hospital, not to be "heroic" or "right" but because it was something that had to be done. I had trouble thinking of my father as book-smart. Like an animal, he relied more on instinct. Which again brings me back to why he left. I would gladly have believed that Duane's father made him disappear and that we were all minor characters in that Greek tragedy Rondo had conjured up, but, more than likely, after my mother's death he was just extremely sad, maybe one of the saddest men who ever lived.

"Boo-hoo!" Rondo said. And I had to agree. "Boo-hoo!"

Kyle and I didn't talk on the way back from the hospital. I couldn't have said much anyway. It was one thing to have been part of the accident, but now too much was happening, too many people were moving in and out of my already muddled head, their loves and hatreds clashing with one another. I just lay on my bed while Kyle worked out. When he was tense, he'd do push-ups until he exhausted himself. He wore plaid boxer shorts and a thin white T-shirt. As he lowered himself, his long black curls touched the floor, the muscles in his shoulders expanding with each breath. That day, he had gone to school and practice, had driven to the hospital, and was still hyped up. I would have offered him a pill but he wouldn't have taken it, his anxiety somehow energizing rather than paralyzing him. I looked away and grabbed one of my books of quotations, famous statements by dead philosophers. Often I'd page through this book, even though I didn't understand most of the quotations, and I finally came to see that a philosopher's job was to explain, in language that was as difficult as possible, that the inexplicable was indeed inexplicable. Consequently, when I read, "After all, is our idea of God anything more than personified incomprehensibility?" I would let its obscurity wash over me, then attempt to translate it into my own words or into an experience. For example, "All knowledge is founded upon the coincidence of an objective with a subjective" equaled "I held a rock in my hand to steady myself." Or "There is no exit from the circle of one's beliefs" meant "I cannot escape from guilt and sorrow." In a way, by tramping through the muddy fields of philosophy, I was attempting to locate myself somewhere between Emily's "Believe!" and Kyle's "Yeah, yeah, yeah." "Here's one," I said to Kyle when he took a break between sets. "'The beautiful is that which pleases universally without a concept.'" He looked up at me, shaking his head, and began another set.

It was about nine o'clock when I went downstairs to get a snack. Aunt Lucy was sitting at the kitchen table with a pile of student papers to her left and a stack of bills to her right. She was still in her dress clothes, a pink silk blouse and a black skirt. She looked tired, the workday and the ordeal of dragging herself through snow draining the color from her face and fading her lipstick.

"How would you like to grade these papers?" she said.

"What are they on?"

"The Declaration of Independence. Why do they give me the document's history when I ask them to tell me what they *think* about it?"

"Because they don't care," I said. I walked into the kitchen and grabbed a spoon and a small container of strawberry yogurt from the refrigerator, then joined her at the table.

"I don't want them to *care*," she said. "I want them to have an opinion."

"About the Declaration of Independence?"

"Why not?"

"Do you know Duane's parents?" I asked, surprising her.

"Yes, I know them. Why do you ask?"

"If I ask you something, will you keep it between us?"

"You mean not tell Kyle?"

"Yeah."

"Why not?"

"Will you?"

"Okay." She put down her pen and placed the paper she was grading back on top of the pile. She took a deep breath, as if she'd been expecting this conversation. "What makes you want to talk about this?"

"Emily told me her parents fight over Mom." I also wanted to tell her Duane's father said he hated Dad and that I'd met Duane's mother, but then I'd have to say when and how.

"They still have fights over her?" she asked.

I nodded.

"I'm not sure what you need to know, but all I can tell you is that her father dated your mother before she met your father." She took a deep breath. "Well, it's more than that. He wanted to marry your mother and couldn't understand why she loved your dad. It got ugly at one point."

"What do you mean?"

"You'd have to know Emily's father to understand. He was very arrogant and rich. A real loose cannon, which made him attractive to a lot of girls but not to your mother. I heard he pulled a knife on your father one night, but I don't know if that's true. You're in high school, you know how things get exaggerated."

"Do you think it was exaggerated?"

"No."

"Why?"

"Because he married a friend of mine. Like us, she wasn't from money, and like your mother, she was very sweet and beautiful. She was really crazy about your mother, and she was a very good artist, but once she met Emily's father, we hardly saw her. I ran into her at the supermarket last summer. She was still beautiful, but it looked like a vampire had sucked the life out of her."

"So that's why you believe the knife story."

"What I do believe is that it's odd we're talking about this. To be honest, I like Emily. She reminds me of your mother because she seems to have escaped that rich-girl entitlement thing I saw every day in high school. But it would have been best if our families had gone their separate ways. Look," she added, "I'm no authority on anything tonight, except the Declaration of Independence, and I certainly don't have any men breaking down my door because of my superb insights, so don't ask me about love."

I thought it was sad she felt that way, and it seemed to me that Kyle was right that we were the reason she wasn't seeing anyone. It was also apparent that this conversation was making her uncomfortable, so I thanked her and went into the kitchen and tossed my empty yogurt container into the garbage.

"We're supposed to get more snow tomorrow," she said as I headed for the stairs. "It's kind of unbelievable, isn't it, like one of those biblical plagues."

Rondo still felt Greek tragedy was more appropriate. The day after I talked to Lucy, he and I snuck off to a room on the third floor above the biology lab, which he had discovered one day when he was late for school and needed a place to hide until the next period. The room must have been the theater department's, because there were painted plywood landscapes resting against the walls and bits and pieces of costumes in boxes or hanging on a metal rack. Dim light filtered in through a small window overlooking the faculty parking lot. Rondo draped a maroon cape fringed with gold tassels over his shoulders and placed a floppy blue felt hat on his head. He collapsed dramatically onto the floor while I paced and related my conversation with Lucy. I also told him about our visit to Duane's and even about the hospital and Kyle's dream.

"He'd kill you for telling me this."

"I have to tell someone," I said. "I'm getting headaches, diarrhea."

"Whoa, I don't need to know everything."

I stood up, feeling a tightness behind my eyeballs, as if I might miss something very important if I blinked. "Is it cold in here?"

"Why don't you wear a cape?" he asked.

I kept pacing. Lately, it had been hard for me to sit still. I took my pills more regularly, but they weren't working. Every morning I felt as if someone were cranking up a volume switch inside my head, as if I were hovering above myself, scrutinizing every one of my movements— pouring cereal, brushing my teeth, opening a book. It was exhausting. I spoke in echoes, sometimes wondering if I was making any sense. When I read, the words might as well have been in a foreign language. "I'm freaking out," I said.

"Dude, just sit down," Rondo said. "I don't know what you want me to say. I mean, this is all very weird stuff. Maybe Duane's old man had your father killed. The guy's evil. I've always thought there was a big black ectoplasm rotting inside Duane's head. Maybe his father got your mother pregnant and Kyle's really his kid, and so Duane and Emily are his brother and sister. That's why I mentioned Greek tragedy. I mean, people live like that. Just turn on Dr. Phil."

"That's not funny," I said.

"Well, what do you want me to say?"

"You know I'm going to start thinking about this stuff now," I said, and I would because Kyle didn't really look like my father, and maybe that was why Duane's father didn't like Kyle going out with Emily, and . . .

Rondo punched me in the arm. "I'm just busting you. You are *soooo* easy to get a rise out of." When the bell rang, he tossed his floppy cap back into the box, along with his cape, then opened the door. "Let's get out of here," he said. As we left the room and tiptoed downstairs, I could hear him whispering behind me, "Evil! Evil! Evil!" And for some reason I laughed.

In this ending, it's still snowing, so hard we wonder if anyone will make it to the game. But this is Buffalo, and people would rather confess to child molestation than miss a sporting event because of snow. We're warming up in what feels like a sauna, the cool bodies and wet clothing mingling with the gym's heat to create a sour smell, so unlike the cold gym we practice in. Not only have people shown up, but the school has had to extend the bleachers to within a foot or two of the court. This is The Game, the one that brings out all the old high school sharpshooters, some relating their heroic moments one more time before returning to their boring lives, others, perhaps more successful, like Duane's father, comfortable just watching the game. But he's here for another reason. Emily hasn't come home for two days, and he's looking for her, wants to talk to and pacify her because she's feeling righteous and good, virtues he vaguely remembers from childhood before some important human connection was severed, and he knows that when people feel righteous, they want to right wrongs, to tell the truth about certain events, and it's a bad time for the truth, seeing that Duane's brain has short-circuited while waiting for Austin Clark to die and that he's stolen a gun from the billiards room, driving by our house one night and firing it twice into the frigid air—"What was that?" Aunt Lucy says, sitting at the kitchen table, and "It's just a backfire from a snow blower," Kyle suggests as Emily squeezes his hand. And her father knows she's been staying with us, but he's afraid to call or to come to the house because of the bruise over her eye, because he'd have to explain how it happened and be the unlikely one to end this tragedy. So here we are, all of us holding our breath as a basketball spins beautifully in the last silent moment before it's tipped to Kyle, who races down court and buries a long three-pointer, all of us suddenly swept up by the flow of the game.

And in this ending, it doesn't matter who wins or who scores how many points, or if Emily has talked to the cops, or if Kyle is her brother—what matters is that through the large exit door under the basket my father has entered the gym. His shoulder-length blond hair spills out of a brand-new Boston Red Sox baseball cap, and he has a bit of a limp and a two-day-old beard. He's wearing jeans and tan work boots, and his red puffy down jacket suggests he lives in a climate of frozen pipes and dead batteries, and no one notices him leaving a minute before the final buzzer, disappearing through the exit doors, ghostlike, before his pain can acquire a shape.

"Do you think this is some kind of movie?" Duane yelled.

We were in the locker room, about to take the floor for the last practice before the championship game. Duane was holding a basketball, standing aggressively over Kyle while Kyle laced and tied his basketball shoes, trying to ignore him. I stepped in between them and said, "Come on, Kyle, let's go," and pulled him by his jersey into the gym, where Father Samuel was shooting short jumpers.

"You guys going to play today?" he said. He was short and squat but still quick for his age.

He had been the point guard on my father's championship team, yet he never had much to say about it. I sometimes wondered if my father even existed or if we all had invented him.

"First some running, gentlemen," Father Samuel yelled, a vein rising from his thick neck, the bright overhead lights reflecting off his bald spot.

The gym was also used for assemblies and school plays, so the seats were cushioned and upholstered, and instead of steps, wide concrete aisles ran from the court to a hall behind the seats. This is where we ran, up and down for a good twenty minutes before returning to the court. As we waited for Father Samuel to divide us into teams, I tried to shake off a chill that had been clinging to me for the last three days, made worse by the gym's frigid temperature. I found myself momentarily floating above everyone, wondering what we were doing here, who these people were, and so on, until someone tossed me a ball and I dribbled it once. That was when I remembered why I played basketball, because if some cosmic joker was really grinning from ear to ear as he viewed me through the sight of his celestial shotgun, then I knew it was certainly harder to hit a moving target, and on a basketball court I was all movement.

It was a good practice, everyone going hard at

one another, especially Kyle and Duane, whom
Father Samuel always paired off, knowing their
history. Halfway through practice Father Samuel's
cell phone rang, and he trotted up one of the
aisles, giving us some plays to run. He wanted
Kyle and Duane to take turns posting each other
up under the basket, and we guards were supposed
to work on different entry passes. But it didn't
take long until Kyle and Duane began banging
into each other, and when Duane straight-armed
Kyle in the back, the drill turned into a wrestling
match. At first Kyle kept cool, backing Duane in,
then shooting fadeaway jumpers or faking Duane
off his feet, drop-stepping, and laying the ball in,
a maneuver my father had worked on endlessly
with him. But then Duane went demonic,
crouching over Kyle like a big blond gorilla, as he
pushed and shoved, one time actually punching
Kyle in the back, which made Kyle wheel to
his left, his elbow catching Duane on the nose
and breaking it, or so we thought as blood fell
to the floor in bright red strings. When Duane
went down on one knee, Kyle made the foolish
gesture of helping him up, leaving himself open
for Duane's right cross that sent him to the floor.
But he was up quickly, and I, for one, believe
that Duane would've killed him if the fight had
continued, but for some reason Duane looked

confused, hesitating, like a finger on a trigger, waiting for a voice to say, "Now." And that was when the sound of someone clapping echoed through the gymnasium. It was Father Samuel, sitting in an aisle seat of the last row of the auditorium. "Your fathers would be pleased," he said, standing and walking toward us.

When I told Rondo about the fight, he said, "Why would you expect normalcy from Father Sam? He was your father's best friend."

"But the whole season could have ended," I said. "Why didn't he break it up earlier?"

"Maybe he had a visitation from God while he was hiding in the last row. Maybe God said, 'Father Sam, let these two boys kick each other's asses. It is my desire and my will. Amen.'"

I laughed but said, "I still don't get it."

"You keep looking for answers, dude, when it's all just movement, backwards and forwards. It's eating and sleeping and screwing, which, personally, I think would ease a lot of your angst. It's the knife, man. Sometimes it sticks, sometimes it doesn't."

He was referring to last summer, when we were at the cemetery, smoking dope, throwing a big bowie knife at a huge oak tree. His father had found the knife in Rondo's brother's bedroom and Rondo had watched him toss it into a garbage can. We played a game, making wishes, hurling the knife at the tree, believing that if it stuck we'd get our wish. "It's a metaphor," Rondo said, and we both nodded, though we were too stoned to explain it. I just wanted to leave, feeling guilty for desecrating my mother's cemetery, imagining her cringing each time the knife struck wood.

First there was my mother, then Aunt Lucy, then came Emily and the woman on the bus, and let's not forget the imaginary one, the girl who goes to bed every night waiting for me to appear in her life. And do I love them? "Love is essentially deception," one of my philosophers writes, and if this is true, then I am one of the great lovers of all time, stalking complete strangers and planning a future with a girl who may not even exist. My mother's love was certainly no deception, my sense of it rekindled every time I grip her paperweights or touch one of her gravestone rubbings. And do I love her? One shrink said I "idealize" her, another that I "mythologize" her, but they didn't know her and couldn't have comprehended the stupidity of their comments. And what of Emily? Is that love a deception? It would be more accurate to call it a

mirage, me being just a necessary worry bringing
her and Kyle closer together. It was my fate to
record their love, even witness the aftermath to their
lovemaking last summer when I stumbled upon
them late morning lying naked on Kyle's bed while
Lucy was off teaching summer school. They were
sleeping, Kyle on his stomach, Emily with her left
leg draped over Kyle's right one, her body tilted so
I could spy her left breast, its brown nipple resting
quietly on Kyle's back, along with her left arm.
Her pink lipstick had been kissed away, and the
bright red nail polish on her fingers hurt my eyes. A
quarter-sized scarlet birthmark on her left buttock
burned like a hot coal, and I walked away somewhat
stunned, promising myself not to tell Rondo for fear
he'd see the experience for what it really was.

The night of the confrontation between Kyle
and Duane I went to bed early, Kyle having
disappeared after dinner into a flurry of yet
another snowstorm. I watched flakes fall and cling
to his pea coat until he appeared to become part
of the storm. Lucy watched with me, concerned
about the bruise on his cheek, asking me how
he got it but not demanding an answer when I
wouldn't say. Then I went to bed, later waking
to a scraping noise, the digital clock reading

12:28. Half-asleep, I staggered downstairs, where I saw Lucy sitting by the kitchen window. Kyle was outside frantically shoveling snow behind him. About eight inches had fallen, and he was nearly done when Lucy knocked on the window, motioning for him to come in. When he did, she made us some tea and asked where he'd been. "I was with Emily," he said.

"At Emily's?" she asked.

"No, *with* Emily," he said. "I know this is hard, but can we talk in the morning?"

"I realize the game's only two days away," she said, "but I've never seen you two like this before."

Kyle's black eyebrows seemed to sag under the weight of secrecy and lies. His left eye was beginning to swell and redden in the corner. "I promise we can talk in the morning," he said. "Just trust me on this."

Lucy sighed and went upstairs mumbling to herself.

When she was out of sight, I took a sip of my tea and asked Kyle where he had really gone.

"He's dead," he said.

"Who?"

"Austin Clark." He hesitated, then corrected himself. "I mean, I think they're both dead. I'm not sure. Emily told me to run, and I did."

Because

Because of the snow.
Because of a hand rising and falling like a hatchet.
Because my mother met my father.
Because my mother met Duane's father.
Because my father locked the door on his way out.
Because a little girl went to school one day.
Because she walked in front of a bus.
Because an apple burns bright in a clear ball of glass.
Because Rondo's knife missed the tree.
Because the woman on the bus would not let me save her.
Because the girl in my dreams would not wake up.
Because Duane's heart was in need of repair.
Because he would not stop until someone died.
Because Emily and my mother were wrong.
Because we are given a face and a name and a fate with
  no because.

Part V

*If it had been possible to build the
Tower of Babel without ascending it,
the work would have been permitted.*
—Franz Kafka

"Who else is dead?" I asked Kyle, wondering what he had to escape from.

He was staring into his teacup, his hair still damp, combed back and tucked behind his ears. "I think I may have hurt Duane, hurt him real bad."

"You mean his nose?"

"No, not that." He looked up at me. "Everything's just unraveling." He didn't say it out of fear, but as if he was sick of our tragedy and glad it was almost over.

"But you said you were with Emily," I reminded him.

"I met her downtown and we went to Friday's. They put us in one of those stupid booths with the TV, and I noticed Emily watching it instead of listening, and the news was on, and that reporter who's been following the accident said Austin Clark died early this morning." He took a deep breath and I thought he was about to cry. "I mean, he's dead. Do you know what that means? It's like I've been doing everything wrong on purpose, so I decided to do something right. Do you believe me?"

"Yes," I said.

"But that asshole Duane must have followed us and seen the same report, because when we left the restaurant he was waiting outside with a stupid bandage over his nose, asking me what I was going to do, so I told him, and he grabbed me and said I was a loser like Dad, and I hit him."

"So he deserved it."

"You don't get it," he said, closing his eyes, grimacing. "I really hit him, like this rush of anger traveled straight from my heart to my hand, and I swear I heard something break inside his head, and he didn't get off the pavement. We shook him, but he wouldn't wake up, and when I looked around, people were staring at me through the restaurant window, and Emily said, 'Just run,' and that's what I did."

I wasn't surprised to hear that Duane had followed Kyle and Emily. It was a family trait. A few days after Emily's father kicked us out of her house, her mother tracked me down. That afternoon, instead of going to practice, I'd met up with Rondo at a coffee shop on Delaware Avenue. As we weaved our way home against a cold wind peppered with flurries, a white Lexus with dark-tinted windows pulled up, slowly keeping pace with us.

"Probably a creep," Rondo said.

But when the window came down, Emily's mother was leaning over, asking if I needed a ride. I said no and explained to Rondo who she was. Sensing an opportunity to live out his older-woman fantasy, he led me over to the car. When we got there, she told Rondo, "Not you. Just him." I hesitated, but Rondo opened the door and pushed me in, backpack and all. He walked away, adjusting his earphones, smiling and singing, as the tinted passenger window closed. I laid my backpack on the floor and told her where I lived.

"I know where you live," she said. "I want to talk."

"I really need to get home."

"Don't worry, you'll get home."

The inside of the car smelled of her perfume, something like oranges, and I imagined her standing in front of a mirror in pink panties and bra, dabbing drops of it behind her ears and on the upper slopes of her small breasts. Although in certain ways I thought of her as being sad and broken, she made me feel strangely alive, for here was a mother, a woman who had given birth and probably loved her children, who was physically breathtaking. I wanted to yell at her and hold her at the same time. But I also wanted to be held, to lay my head on her breasts and inhale her scent. I wanted her to stroke my head and make everything go away. I became so confused that my body involuntarily jerked forward, and I asked to be let out of the car. She pulled into someone's driveway.

"You okay?" she asked.

"I just need to walk," I said.

"I know the feeling." She reached for her purse in the back seat. "You want a Xanax?"

"I have my own pills."

She laughed. "We sure are a pair." She faced the windshield, grasping the wheel with two hands, taking a deep breath. "Let's start all over," she said, and when I looked at her she seemed stronger, more alert. She put on some classical music, backed out of the driveway, and drove in the general direction of where I live. At that moment she could have been anyone's mother, picking up her son from basketball practice. I thought our little drama was done until she veered into the entrance of the park, driving right by the scene of the accident.

After we finished our tea, Kyle and I sat up until five in the morning, trying to decide what to do. I knew Rondo's parents were in Aruba for a week, so I called him, and when he said to come over, we left Lucy a note and caught a bus to Rondo's. There was only one old drunk sleeping in the back of the bus, surrounded by a number of empty bags from fast-food restaurants, as if this was the last ride of a long, cold night. I wondered what dramas the driver had seen or overheard during his shift and if our sad story would have shocked him. Before we left home, Kyle had called Emily to discover that Duane had regained consciousness at the restaurant, ending up with a headache and an itch for revenge. I was beginning to think you could shoot Duane in the head with a silver bullet and he wouldn't die, yet his recovery, coupled with Emily's promise to meet us at Rondo's, put us in a better mood. Still, we couldn't get past Austin Clark's death, and his spirit seemed to ride in the seat behind us. We had touched him during his last semiconscious moments, and his life was not unlike ours—a combination of catastrophes and dumb decisions. Moreover, we sensed, without yet knowing, that his death would forever change our future, that we would never again forget how unpredictable life was.

Emily's mother guided the Lexus to the same curb that Duane had jumped while driving us into the baseball field just a few nights before. We parked in a spot where kids made out on weekends but which right now was occupied by a father and his two small sons constructing a snowman by the baseball backstop. We watched them for a moment, not saying anything. Then she turned slightly toward me, seeming almost embarrassed that she had brought me here. "You really do look like your mother," she said. She leaned over and I thought she was going to grab my leg, but she opened the glove compartment and removed a metal flask encased in black leather. She unscrewed the top and took a sip, then offered me some. "What do you know about me and your mother?" she asked.

"Only what my aunt Lucy told me," I said, tasting her lipstick as I drank from the flask, feeling my insides warm up.

"You probably won't believe me, but I miss Lucy," she said, reaching for the flask.

"Then why did you stop being her friend?"

She laughed. "Because I wasn't allowed to see her."

"Because of your husband?"

"Oh, that would be too simple. Your father was a bullhead, too. He knew how to push my husband's buttons, though they probably would've been friends if it weren't for your mother."

"My mother?"

"She was a hard act to follow," she said, taking another sip. "I loved her, but she was almost too good. It was fine if you were a man, but as a woman you always felt somehow diminished in her presence."

"I'm sorry," I said.

"I would prefer you'd be sorry for Duane," she said, surprising me. She screwed the cap onto the flask and settled it back into the glove compartment. "I know what Duane is," she said. "He was born angry, and his father nurtured that rage. But he's my baby, just like you were your mother's."

"And you want me to do what?"

"Just let it die. You know my husband will take care of you. I know how terrible that sounds, but I think your mother would have agreed with me."

The car was becoming colder and the windows began perspiring from the heat of our conversation. I was about to tell her that my mother had been dead for so long I couldn't imagine how she would have reacted to our dilemma, and that I've never been able to stop Kyle from doing anything. I wanted to say that there was nothing left but to wait until spring and return to my tower. But all possibilities vanished with a pounding on the driver's side window. She hit a switch, and we watched the tinted window slowly descend.

My head was resting on a window when the bus came to a sudden stop, waking me and Kyle.

"You told me this was where you wanted to

get off," the bus driver said. He looked tired, though happy his shift was about over, grabbing his hat from a nearby hook as if rehearsing his exit. I reached for my backpack, which contained a few days' change of underwear and socks, and then Kyle and I jumped off the bus and watched it pull away. The snow had stopped falling and lay unshoveled, creating a field of white, and the sky was clearing for the first time in almost a week, the sun poking its head over the top of a chimney.

"A blue sky," I said to Kyle, putting the knapsack on my back.

"It must be a mirage."

We walked down the street until we came to Rondo's house, a huge colonial with multiple chimneys and a tall iron gate guarding the driveway. The front door opened and Rondo stood in the doorway, squinting, wearing a light blue bowling shirt, tan shorts, and blue flip-flops. A baseball hat worn backwards kept his earphones in place. All that was missing was a pair of sunglasses. "Dudes," he yelled, waving his hands over his head as we opened the gate and trudged through the snow.

It was Emily's father poking his head through the window like a cop, his features so distorted he appeared to be wearing a mask. I wondered how long he'd been following us and what he thought we were up to, though he didn't seem jealous. More likely he was mad that his wife had sought me out and that for a brief moment he wasn't the boss.

"I told you to stay home," he said to her. "I told you I'd take care of things." I could see his big black Volvo idling next to us. His wife looked embarrassed, staring into the steering wheel, and I didn't understand why she didn't respond. He thrust his face closer, his mouth no more than three inches from hers. "As usual, you're screwing things up," he said.

"It was my fault," I said, surprising myself, wondering if in some odd way I had created the situation by getting into the car.

"Who asked you?" he said. He reached in to grab me, but his wife pushed his arm away. "Beat it," he said, and I opened my door, reached for my backpack, and stepped into about a foot of snow.

"Shit," I said, looking up at his large frame towering over the hood. He was dressed for work—blue topcoat, tan scarf, white shirt, red tie. I had a notion to throw a snowball at him.

"I'm not going to leave him freezing in the snow," his wife said.

His head disappeared back into the window.

"You'll do what I tell you to do," he barked.

I looked at her before closing the door. "I'm all right," I said. "I can walk from here." I threw my backpack over one shoulder, high-stepping out of the snow into the street. I jogged for a few minutes, not looking behind me, remembering Duane shooting us the finger when he abandoned us on that fateful night. I decided to do the same.

At about noon, lying on a pullout couch in Rondo's basement, I awoke to laughter and a loud crash. "Strike!" Rondo yelled, adding, "Wake up, sleepyhead." I rolled over, listening to the clang of the automatic pin-setter as it cleared the alley and to the hum of a bowling ball rolling its way back. I sat up slowly, trying to remember why I was here, which wasn't hard once I spied Emily and Kyle drinking Cokes over by the wet bar. Their hair was damp from showering, and they were wearing matching gold bowling shirts. Rondo left the lane and walked toward me, tossing a bright red bowling shirt into my face. It had the name *Red* stitched over the pocket. "Hey, Red," he said, "why don't you take a shower and put this on." Even Emily and Kyle laughed.

After I showered and changed, I caught up with them in the kitchen making sandwiches. It all

seemed surreal: four kids in bowling shirts sharing
a huge empty house, trying for a few minutes
to forget that one person was dead, another was
injured, and still others were looking for them.
For sure, a bit scary but also exhilarating, as if I
had a purpose besides just existing, as if this role
had been waiting for me all along. And in spite of
having no place to go and no idea what to do, I felt
oddly in control and somewhat dangerous.

We sat quietly eating until Kyle said, "We've
decided to go to the cops, but I promised I'd talk
to Emily's father first."

"Why?" I asked.

He took a sip of milk. "Because he says he
knows where Dad is."

"And you believe him?"

Rondo laughed and walked out of the kitchen,
Kyle following him with his eyes. "What choices
do we have?" he said to me.

"I don't know, but I don't trust him."

"I don't either," Emily said.

When Rondo came back into the kitchen, he
was swinging a key ring around his index finger.
"I'll take you there," he said, "but then I leave.
This isn't my battle, okay?"

In the early hours of the morning, my father sits

in the Bonanza bus station with a traveling bag on his lap and a ticket for New York City in his hand. He wants to stay but knows he can't take care of himself, much less two young boys. He rubs the ticket between his fingers, worrying it until the letters are smudged. He goes to the bathroom and splashes water onto his face. *Raiders Rule* is scrawled in red marker in the bottom right corner of the mirror, a reference to a local street gang. The last sound he remembers is the hiss of the doors before the bus swallows him up.

Or maybe he decides to stay at a local motel for a few days, thinking the pain will go away and a plan will emerge. He has withdrawn enough cash to get by, and he uses the money to take a cab that periodically drives by the house. In the motel room he drinks hard liquor and does push-ups on a cheap orange rug. He watches TV or sometimes just sits on the bed staring at a bad painting of a bowl of fruit. One night he goes to a bar and meets a truck driver who offers to take him to the West Coast. Outside of Cleveland, in the middle of a snowstorm, he wants to be near her possessions, her clothes, her paperweights, her perfume, but he can't bring himself to say, "Drop me off here"; he can't admit he's made a terrible mistake. He buys a postcard at the next truck stop and addresses it to his older son, but ends up keeping it in his back pocket, where it will fade and decompose in a washing machine somewhere in the middle of Iowa. In California, he pumps gas and works at convenience and liquor stores, one time even picking grapes with migrant workers, who don't ask questions. Living under a strange sun in an even stranger geography, he eventually forgets who he is, his one last glimpse occurring while watching a thin black kid dribble a basketball over the wide cracks of an inner-city asphalt court.

Or maybe something darker. Maybe after shoveling he changes his clothes and drives to an all-night diner where he and his wife used to go after high school dances. He's sitting in a booth, sipping black coffee from a small white cup, imagining past conversations with her, wondering why they didn't come here after their children were born, thinking of all the things they should have done. He remembers how her smile could ignite a room, and he's about to ask the waitress for a refill when an old man in a ragged topcoat, his face spotted with dried blood, stumbles through the diner's front door, shouting, "I was at Pearl Harbor when the Japs attacked. All hell broke loose in the mess hall," saying it over and over again, until he gives the old man a twenty-dollar bill and leaves. He sits in his car for a moment, seeing his future in the old man's face, and it's not long before daybreak, so he drives the car home, then boards a bus back to downtown and another to Niagara Falls. He buys another cup of coffee at the bus station there, listening to the city awaken, then pays a cabbie to take him to the American side of the Falls. The cab stops outside the entrance, which is closed. "They won't open until ten," the cabbie says, but he gets out anyway and tells the driver to leave. No need to mention the cold, or the long walk through the snow as a blinding light leads him to the river's edge, only a half mile from the roar and mist that's rising into the heavens. No need to mention how he collapses in knee-deep snow, watching the rapids pound huge boulders kicked up from the river's bottom. No need to mention the voices in his head or his last memory of being tossed through a spectrum of colors, waiting for the hand of God—which of course never comes—to reach out and save him.

"I'd go with the last story," Rondo says. "Definitely the last one."

In this ending, there's no basketball game. The gym is overflowing with spectators, but there are no teams. No one will show up to the game late and hit the winning shot; no one will throw the ball into the stands and sneak out a locker-room window. No one—out of guilt, or sorrow, or love—will return to ask for forgiveness. Just a lot of noise, overheated spectators, bright lights, and a high school band priming the audience for a grand finale that will never come.

"That's Lucy's car," I said as we pulled into Emily's driveway.

"I don't like this," Emily said. "You don't know what he's capable of. Let's just go to the police."

"I'm with her," Rondo said.

"And leave Lucy here?" Kyle reminded us. He grabbed Rondo's arm. "Listen, you've helped enough. Just go home."

When Rondo left, we walked toward the house, the front door opening as we neared it. Emily's mother greeted us in jeans and without makeup, telling us to go into the billiards room, where Emily's father was waiting. We found him on a stool at the wet bar, balancing a rum and Coke on his palm. "This is becoming a bad habit," he said. He wore tan corduroys, running shoes, and a dark blue turtleneck sweater. Combined with his graying red hair and jovial expression, the outfit made him look very Christmassy, as if he had been waiting patiently to give us a present. Duane sat next to him with a small piece of gauze taped over the bridge of his nose. He must have just gotten home, because he was still warming his hands in the pockets of his black pea coat. Off to his right, Aunt Lucy sat on the couch where we had received our first warnings. Emily's mother joined her.

"You said you knew where our father was," Kyle said.

I saw Emily frown and shake her head.

"Who?" Emily's father said, and we realized we had been duped.

Kyle looked at Lucy. "How much did he tell you?"

"About the accident, everything," she said.

"Well, it probably wasn't true."

"You never get it, Kyle," Emily's father said. "It doesn't matter what's true or what really happened. All that matters is what we're going to do about it." He seemed calm in contrast to Duane, who jumped off the stool and began pacing around the pool table, as if we weren't in the room. He was taking deep breaths, and even his father seemed perplexed by his behavior.

"I'm going to the police," Kyle said, which made Duane stop pacing.

"I've already explained why that won't work," Emily's father said.

Aunt Lucy stood. She looked very athletic in

her jeans, knee-high leather boots, and red ski jacket. "He's doing the right thing," she said, moving toward us, gesturing for us to leave.

"No one's going anywhere," Emily's father said, banging his drink onto the wet bar and approaching us. His wife intercepted him, and when she told him to stop, he pushed her to the floor.

Lucy went to her aid and Emily said, "Oh, Daddy!" Meanwhile I was about to jump him when Duane mumbled something unintelligible and pulled out a handgun from one of his pockets. He pointed it at Kyle and said, "Maybe you," and then at his father, "Or maybe you," and then placed the barrel of the gun to his own temple, "Or maybe me," adding, to his father, "You wouldn't mind that, would you." He seemed more agitated than anything, or hurt, or sad. In short, he didn't look like Duane.

His father stared at him with the kind of amusement he might have saved for a particularly difficult business associate, as if he were sizing up the situation, weighing the possibilities, very aware that a bullet in Duane's head would indeed solve a lot of problems. Noticing his father's expression, Duane raised the gun above him and fired one round into the ceiling. It sounded like the blast of a lightning bolt, and I waited for the small hole it left to generate a crack that would sever the room in two. Duane fired again, his arm recoiling, this second shot appearing to calm him. He lowered the gun and sat down on the floor, and his mother came to console him. His father just laughed, shaking his head, and Aunt Lucy said, "Let's go." As we left the billiards room, Emily's father said to Emily, "You, too?" and her mother said, "Just let her go. I mean it." He laughed again, shaking his head in disgust.

Outside, the sky was clear and the sun so bright it turned the new snow into a mirror, so that one could imagine some benevolent god gazing down thoughtfully on his own reflection.

After we got back from the police station I had a long nap, not waking until after dusk. I went downstairs, but no one seemed to be home. I leafed through a pile of mail on the dining room table and saw an envelope addressed to me. It was from the zoo. My request to adopt the African Wild Ass had been approved. Enclosed was an information sheet on the animal and a decal, along with a letter stating that my name would be in the zoo's Adopt-An-Animal brochure.

I stuffed all the information into my back pocket and went into the kitchen, walking toward the sink to wash my hands. Through a window, I could see Kyle standing near a garbage can, squirting something into it. When he lit a match and dropped it into the can, a huge flame illuminated the cold night, then settled into a slow burn. I grabbed my jacket and joined him, peering into the can. It was empty except for two smoldering old basketball shoes.

"Why didn't you tell me you'd kept them?" I asked.

"I don't know," he said, warming his hands over the fire.

We lingered there until the fire burned itself out. Then Kyle put his arm around me and led me back to the house.

This is the part of the story where I'm supposed to say what happened to everyone: that Duane was arrested and eventually transformed into a decent human being, that his father was charged with obstruction of justice and lost his business, that his wife got an apartment and devoted herself to painting and to her daughter and to her friendship with Lucy, that Emily never saw her father again and didn't miss the nice clothes or fancy cars or expensive vacations, that we came to see Lucy more as a mother than an aunt, all of us creating the kind of family we'd always wanted, and that Kyle and I escaped harm because we came forward and did, as Kyle said, "the right thing." In short, the kind of ending insisting on a reward for kind and just actions. The kind of ending demanding that we trust in some ultimate plan or logic, even in the Great Chain of Being.

And there's some truth to this ending, because we have become closer with Lucy, and we weren't held accountable for Austin Clark's death. But facts remain: that evil does exist, that the rich rarely get punished for their actions, that Emily's mother wasn't strong enough to leave her husband, that my mother would forever be dead and my father absent, and that if there is a Grand Plan, its logic, at least for now, escapes me.

Yet I am sure of one thing: it is late spring and I am standing at the top of my tower with Kyle and Emily, a cool Canadian breeze cleansing our faces. Enormous white clouds are blowing in off the lake, and I am no longer afraid. I have trust in Kyle and Lucy, and in the power of certain images—a rust-colored paperweight, a gravestone rubbing, two basketball shoes smoldering in a garbage can on a cold January night, a clock with no hands. How they cling to us, offering some kind of consolation, like these tiny sailboats just now quivering on the surface of the lake, bobbing up and down like seagulls, yet never going under.

Believe. Believe.